S I T U

STEVEN SEIDENBERG

ALSO BY STEVEN SEIDENBERG

Pipevalve: Berlin

Null Set

Itch

S I T U
by Steven Seidenberg

B L A C K   S U N   L I T
BROOKLYN   NEW YORK

Black Sun Lit
c/o Jared D. Fagen
195 Underhill Ave., #2A
Brooklyn, NY 11238

www.blacksunlit.com
editors@blacksunlit.com

Printed in the United States of America by Bookmobile

www.bookmobile.com

Distributed by Small Press Distribution

1341 Seventh Street
Berkeley, CA 94710

www.spdbooks.org

PRAISE FOR *S I T U*

To engage with the narrative flow of Steven Seidenberg's *Situ* is to pass through the looking glass of consciousness into a seriocomic world of "mnemonic throes" and "the null of place." I think, therefore where am I? And what? And when? We feel the phenomenal world slip-sliding away, even as we marvel at the charged field of language and thought thus brought to light.

—Michael Palmer, author of *The Laughter of the Sphinx*

Steven Seidenberg has confected a stanza out of trains of thought that falter as explanation turns on itself too many times to grasp. He gives us the most amiable of mad narrators who twists gorgeous epistemological filigree, never escaping "captive selfdom" as the lonely audience of his own powerful articulation, an "inner other." *Situ* is the fruit of the philosophical quest: a horror of the body—"face flush with the rancid muck that covers his cadaver"—and the rational mind in its infinite regress. "The point" is to capture the moment of knowing—the happy ending where truth is completely expressed. But the unknown overwhelms the known as it becomes known as unknown, a terrain hidden between what can and can't be said. This terrain is full of wonder, tenderness, laughter, failure, chatter. Our narrator enlarges it by increments as each stanza glides inexorably to its cliff. He hurls us over, only to start again with new faith in hundreds of fresh beginnings.

—Robert Glück, author of *Jack the Modernist*

A feat of extreme smarts, folding in iterative density and intense decay, *Situ* does philosophy as labyrinthine lit. It's the private demo of an *unheimlich* maneuver, a novel of raveling, a vagrant meditation, with its protagonist assuming a metaphysical/mind-body position (bent over himself, inverted) that leads to a voyage around his brume, a roam of his own. This is outsider metaphysics, insider epistemology, inside-out methodology, limning limits of knowledge, will, action, language, memory, and unity in the creation, the *scansion*, of self and world. Literalizing notions of ground and point of view, and elaborating an abstract analytical baroque, a syntactical sublime, and an abject disoriented philosophy, Seidenberg creates a novel of *sui generis* reduction, full of dark, dreck humor, deep obsessional disorder, and relentless musical propulsion. Its intestinal yet Latinate formalism, its agonistic wit and ruinous wonder, its keen bent for passivity, would make Beckett chortle, Husserl mull, Descartes nod, Spinoza correspond, Melville wax fanciful. An original, gutsy book.

—Mina Pam Dick, author of *Delinquent*

φ

But that's not all. This seat, *his* seat, has never been another's, has always only been dispensed to find his occupancy near. To suit his nearing occupation, if not the present circumstance of being thereby occupied, of being set upon by only him, by him alone. This is to say that as he turns his gaze back to his harbor, no matter what corrosive goad provoked him to dethrone, the cardinal intimation that his pulp should find no lading on that ramshackle recliner leaves him hardly an existence—hardly corrigibly *extant*—a manifold of carrion both drifting past and soon to come, and soon to spoil *here…*

φ

Surely it has happened before, he thinks, he has left his bench before, many times, *countless* times, which does nothing to prevent him from attempting such a count, an assay that's near equal to the feint of its achievement, at least when it's considered from the outside, or…the outside of the outside, *nearly* the inside, but not quite—not yet—*he* still knows the difference…knows the difference is *all* difference, every difference held in state both in and out, in state and kind…

φ

There was that one occasion, just the other day, he can almost feel the weight of the sun on his back...It was the last sun, the last time there was a sun, that the weight of the back of the sun was...He can almost taste it, that's what they say—that's what *they say* they say, he thinks—that one can almost taste it, when one thinks that one can taste it...But that's not right...not quite *his* right, if nothing less obscure...He thinks that if he manages to disregard all other sense—the less of it, the more of it, he thinks it could be all—then he can nearly cast *himself* back into that last phoebus, perhaps the brightest double yet to simper through the burnished vault, the vaulting bar...

φ

Just the other day. The other day, when he had, for example, left his bench for nothing less than the necessity of leaving his bench, and nothing more perhaps, again perhaps, perhaps again...For nothing more or less than the necessity of leaving his bench, an urgency made manifest by nothing more or less than the perplexed and blushing affect of his calentured cheek, his lips adrift from gums in pained retraction from the glossa, and the next ostensive centering of everything that centers on a muscular convulsion of the egress, of the split...

φ

But no, he thinks, not yet, or not again, he'd rather vow; it's always best when yet is made indifferent to again, when one can't tell the difference—when the difference is indifferent—and yet again is again yet...always when what has not happened nonetheless rescinds its dun opprobrium of losses and returns that fevered omphalos to some intrinsic innocence of gusts...Perhaps it was the wind made spit to transpierce his latissimus, perhaps his mast fit witless to the porch of his arrival, but—it's so he sees, he sees it's so, for once he can attend the rule, and this time, just this once, not merely sharp his eager focus on the absence of a speaker, of a speaker spoken to by speaking out...

φ

There was a sun the other day, he felt its weight upon his back, but even in the living of that moment he still failed to think...still *rightly* failed to think that mass an attribute of anything but his deferred reception, of his burden in its hauling, a fantasy of ballast that seemed sweet as it reached tongue. If he cannot taste it, he cannot bear it—an endless source of trouble in his commerce on the boulevard, however one can say that he has bought or sold his wares. If he cannot taste it...

φ

It is not his, this foundling glimpse, but everything that's in it is imputable to him. He cannot think this protean reduction of the scene to some assemblage of distrait associations—of surrenders of the outside to some intimated core—accordingly a predicate of his peculiar potency, his binding resignation to a boundless drive, a soughing dray, but who is really able to make such returnless venture allege a conformation to a vision of achievement, so a practice in the slightest way compelled? An odd rhetorical; who's to say anything...to speak anyway...

φ

Thus accepting his unknowing—if unknowable—acceptance of a world that's not on offer but is taken up by force,
the sense of sensibilities not understood as sensate allows
a nearer vision of his present paralipsis, of what he thinks
a vestige of his *minderless* lookout. Nearer is not inside,
it may be, but there's the triumph; to be inside would be
equal to a positure bemused. If it's inside that you're after,
then it's inside…

φ

Thus *revealing* his acceptance of a world he thinks as given,
of a world he's since received…he's since *aroused*, if still
too soon, he thinks back to the last sun, the only sun he's
managed to think back to as a likeness, but still he can't lay
claim to having ever claimed it present, so to here fulfill his
promise…his next promise to the absent…

φ

How else could one model such an aftermath of voices?
How return one's thinking to a day so long ago? So long
past? Return such empty savor to the trick of having past?
Why not here allow this indiscretion—this *offensive*—to
take one no less willingly than bound towards such presentiment…towards some resolve that's set *before* the passions
of the scene to come? To come, it is to come, he thinks, but
that is not his present purpose, nor is it…

φ

The last sun, the only sun, the only is the last sun, and that
past long or short ago, whenever it played out within his
in, it doesn't matter…Whether it matters or not, that is to
say, he knows it can't be known, if for no other reason than

the fact that such a standard is precisely what's gone missing since it happened, since it last appeared...

φ

Without this subjugation to the discrepating shadows—some atmospheric median to *measure up against*—he knows that he can't hope to frame the passage of the hours, and without the passing hours his days appear a nearly insurmountable expanse. Perhaps he *can* hope, but *he* doesn't; for him it's proved impossible to cite what he's collected as a singular impression—as a summary dissemblance—without the sense of passing into typic pose. He remembers only that which is inestimably long ago, for the fact that if the estimate were obvious to him—and that is all that *means*, he thinks, that viscerous alterity of cherished modes, of modes *held dear*—then he'd recall the figure of such gustatory *ignis* whenever it had slithered into happenstance, so had at some present time appeared...

φ

All this to elucidate his wholly novel status...his *displacement* from the outside of the inside of the view, a posture unexampled to the auditors of fortune as they're passing, as they saunter quickly past his septic cipher of a seal. He is as yet none other than another, than no *other* other ought... not only as *an* other, but as *all* others, as every other ever ought to be. That some are is as others ought is not his pressing problem, but of him...but *for* him...

φ

Enough. He's had enough. But such conditional satiety won't dissuade him from returning to a moment from which he'll soon forever more depart, when once again the burden of a passing fancy passes into dilatory savor, the radiance coerce a squint from convalescent pupils and the heat upon his neck impel the sweat to start...

φ

He can still recall that day as clearly as...as clear as this one, but he can *see* it clearer; it's not that it's more proximate, but that it's limned in greater detail, as a spotlight can illumine in an instant what's been hidden from the easy eye for centuries. When was it, he wonders...no, that's not the crucial question, not the *right* question, he's sure. Even he—*despite* his longings—will not foist upon his subjects the vexation of such trivial concerns. Or perhaps that's not the reason. Rather rather. Rather rather than perhaps...

φ

He is yet rather incapable of saying...of *deducing* when it was that he was last, perhaps still first, but *surely* last... when he was last afflicted with that menacing exigency, that cavalcade of poses that his plethora implies. It would be foolish to assume the contradiction has escaped him, that such contraction of cross purposes—cross *explanations*, he believes, as though he might *esteem* his dreaming motive into some triumphant portrait of conditions not just born out, but derived—could slip by without notice, not by tongue or affectation but by being likewise thrust into an unshared world...It would be *foolish*, he accepts, and while such foolishness won't push his expedition into shipwreck, he feels it as a shot across the prow...

φ

And neither is his *pleasure* what excites such restive purpose, what instigates his suppliance to such a feckless trove. *No* pleasure, really. He confesses to no pleasure in the pleasing, but in his image of the *being pleased*...

φ

He has this once remembered...has *suggested* to his alter, if only just this moment having first inferred its gaze, that his facile acquiescence to this inchoate adventure may be twofold, but in each case feigns the one...the *singular* surrender to...

φ

Need he go no further? No, that's still not it, he thinks, not as it's most liable to engender such resolve. Need he make it clearer, more like such a one would fairly suffer in return? It's always been a posture of passivity he's after, a threshold of *receivership* he ambles ever *towards*...Need such a hapless seity go anywhere, he wonders? No, there is no need, it goes without saying; there is no need to say it, but what's more...

φ

One need not say one need not say, he can't help but remember, a fact that won't prevent him from attending to that standard for the equally impertinent, but no less circumstantial...*does not ever* thus prevent him from the saying for the exploit of disclosing that what needs be said is nothing...nothing like what *is* said, which is always as a surfeit, the always more than nothing that this symbol of an absence makes intrinsic, makes a predicate; the vessel that each more than merely nothing serves to fill...

φ

He has unconcealed a twofold explanation for his rancor—his subtle divagation, as a parenthetic pause; he has
recalled that at his earliest awareness of the sun upon his
shoulder, his neck, his back, the back of his neck and the
front of his shoulder, as felt through spreading gelatin of
grimy frock, of molting peel...that the advent of the shine
through that imperious edema stirred him from his resting
place to seek out some relief. To seek an ease from what
had seemed a *visceral* distemper, accorded by the fevered
cusp of spitting lips, of guts clenched tight...

φ

So which is it, he wonders, which point for the pointer, for
the pointer to point to as his foundling husk, his ported
shell? It is easy enough to accept the occasional coincidence of sun and seizure without designating primacy of
stimulus or cause, but it is just as easy to deem *either* the
occasion...the *placeholder* of a world expelled from aspiration or expectancy, a world that's been unyieldingly...
interminably deferred. Deferred to present circumstance,
that is...that is the presence...

φ

Deferred to present circumstance, that *then* of spendthrift
splendor—both writ across his rictus and the vizard of the
star—was made at last at least to seem an equal approbation
for this consummate remainder, this submission to an otherwise *importunate* regard. Just who's being importuned, who
being importuned...

φ

One thinks of every circumstance as serving some base ego, some target of intention that is consummately in, which is to say—not out...*He* thinks of every mover as a person-hood, an agent, whereas the seeming obverse is not graced with such resort. Not every fitful anima is likewise capable of movement but...In *this* case both coincident conditions—the fever that ingeminates the out that mirrors in, and the in that takes the mood of every out to be its own—are identically engrossing, and together serve as setting for this portent of a finished tale. Or that one, he thinks. That one that he thinks *of*, and not in...

φ

And so it was that *when* the sun was last lit blear and bold, when last his weary rapture hit that muzzle of a gloam, and not because of, not by virtue...He slackens and he hesitates, he fractures every fractured stone, and there, just there, he seizes on an inkling of some next propitious advent, a supplicant's peremptory refrain. He recalls that pulsing plenitude because it was quite blinding, because that gasping vault was so discordantly ablaze, but that's not why he's stumbled into that same recollection, why he can't seem to stop himself from yielding to this swoon. For that he has himself to blame. In that, he finds his witness...

φ

But that's not it at all, he thinks, that's not his it at all. Or while that's not *not* it at all, that's still not it, and it's always just the shibboleth of this perplexed anaphora he's after. That it. This that. That this it...

φ

What matters is...what *is* the matter is, that is, is that that once...that once before...that at least once before he left his bulwark unattended, precisely as he had at some pass prior to this last return, and that time, while perhaps still something less than...or is it more...either more *or* less than singular in occurrence—not unique, that is to say, in his typology of forms—is nonetheless the only instant...*the one instance* of abandon he can actually remember, or in what he imagines as a present tense recall...

φ

That one last time the sun was out, and inside he could feel his bloat amount to an exigency, a want, he is convinced, that no consumer of like character can fail to fully slake without...Without at once erupting, in the strain of abnegation; without discretely bursting, before the next pass through...

φ

He knows this is a commonplace, in his life as all others; he knows that recollecting just *this* instance is inane. What matters is that in his view the *present* scene is singular, and that not for the reference to his past evacuations, but the length of time it took him to retreat to place and prime; that in all other incidents of leaving off by leaving place his leaving had no consequence—achieved no signal anomie, thus adduced neither discomfort nor ensuing palliation to apportion with a logic, or a cause...

φ

That he can only recollect one previous occurrence of the kind might prove a fault in his analysis, but it's a point of scant relation to what concerns his...what concerns *him* here and now. Which is the understanding...the *drawing out* of what in substance made his stray from course result in such ponderous dudgeon, in refractory *replacement*—a change in state accepted, if in any tense endured. If revealed at any moment that's conceived of as at present; as having been—or *soon to be*—described in present term. To catch the nervy beast one must not spring out at a distance...

φ

What makes such recall apropos, thus different from all others—from that of any *other* other, next to or to come—is that *he has it*, and so can give a shape to that lost movement *in the now*. This is not to say that what on this deferred occasion has acceded to the mind's eye—or even on that very same occasion this occasion here evokes—is what there was...is *exactly* what there was when it was there, there on the outside, but only that such aggregate bears some obscure proximity to what he thinks there is or was... there was or is...

φ

Perhaps it is a *kind* of saying—a modulation of no small consequence. Perhaps he is saying *to himself* what he believes does not corroborate such cursory...such *uniform* reversion to some singular momentum neither distant now nor near, as refuse bobbing on the waves that catches the regard of idle gazer so that, following, the speed of what had once appeared the chaos of the deluge reads as stagnant in relation to the moving shore. He is saying to *himself* that thus distinguishing the torrent—thereby bringing it to stasis, if not *keeping it in view*—does not confirm...should not *betoken* the singularity of anything but a detail in the bracket of attention, where before…where before that there was no such, there was none…

φ

There have been times, he thinks, and thinks it with a confidence unsourced in evidentiary display…There have been times, he knows, not knowing any reason he should know them so…

φ

There have been times before *this* insurmountable regression—times when he had left his harbor just as nonchalantly, though only one such previous example leaps to mind. And that, it seems assured, is only sure on this occasion for a preternatural deference to some other sort of praxis—or perhaps of the same sort, but in some future sort of mull—when his quondam discomposure will with similar imperative require him to quit his place and so relieve his bloat…

φ

There is no such directory he'd like to now endeavor— that he'd ever like to now pursue as any patent end—and for this no pursuer would be less likely to thank him, if he could in the midst of his habitual aversion keep control over the impulse to do as he would *want* to now avoid. It can't be much of a surprise that one so full of virtue— so wholly virtuous, he thinks, as though he need remind himself—would conscientiously distrust the capricious pulse of longing, and in order to ensure he doesn't rashly follow whimsy in the face of this predicament—that he won't fail to understand what led him lurching lengthwise into this most thrilling spate—he's inclined to purpose forward towards his full disinclination, an easement somehow palpably...*intractably* his own...

φ

That the glint of shining rill...the shining rill of coruscations should impregnate his mute sputter of a credo with mimesis—with a clarity that mirrors the illuminated detail of that always thought as sedentary *mise-en-scene*...That the clarity of detail in the bracketing of portions—in each compelled distinction that seems inner as its own—should more probably engender the recurrence of that savor—well, the trouble with imputing cause to some fixed correspondence seems implicit, so expressing it inane...

φ

Yes, it is more pleasant; he commands a zealous *taste*, that is, for even *sparse* illumination; he'd happily solicit *any* tawdry torch to brighten up his gloom. But why would such impulsive inclination effect purpose? Why does it matter that he likes the play of sunlight on his vistas, that the void should seem to open with this impudent *élan*? Does pleasure play a role in any comparable recurrence? Can one only recapitulate what one has first enjoyed? And most importantly, perhaps, in hopes of searching out a witness...a *testament* to what he here unerringly presumes, does the mist of bruising skies deprive the world of focused detail? Does limpidity revealed and then occluded still purport no more a loss of what was there, set in the sun? Is there not a clarity to even *blurred* horizons? Is there motive to believe the clearest detail *the most real*...

φ

That the light revealed, that is, not as refraction of a dappled world but of an *inner* stasis, of everything not as it is, but as one thinks it will. Why should such lucidity be prudent to the nature of the thingness it puts forward as a forward? Why not take the haptic mists of some occluded starscape—some ruin of fog and clouds rent from the sky—for precisely that precision, but as such in the limning of an image of the blear? Is a preference for lucidity...for the glinting gold putrescence of a gloating star enough to justify some claim to rectitude, to *discernment*—that only in that focus can the truth find its villein? What leaning is, what preference is— it's all too much to hazard. What he wants to know is where the foundling present finds its presence, in what perfervid slither into fistule, into void...

φ

It seems to him that even this indomitable litany of rhetoricals requires more than isolation in the thingness of the thing as it appears; that every passing moment, regardless of its character—every image of the gilded fields transposed upon the plough—is indentured to duration *through* its presence, through the total that displays it as a picture of what's now what's yet to be revealed...

φ

If any world endures *as such* it can't be in an instant; its passage through the present must extend both to and fro. Think, he thinks, a knot of string split loose upon the pavement, imagine its frayed ends unfurled across the boundless marl; watch it trailing off, while firmly fastened to *this* nodule, an omphalos he tries to think as infinitely small, but he can't do it, he just can't, and so his insight takes this form; that the infinite extension of the future, contrary to accepted trust—and it seems to him a common precept, even if it's here professed as some form of digression, as an unexampled subtlety, an *evanescent* leap—is not mirrored in a focus without meter, without substance; a limit whose ostensive pith is proffered as a traipse across...

φ

But metaphors alone, he thinks, suggest such meager prospect he wishes there were something like a bit of twine in sight—something other than his thinking thoughts to succor as a purpose in the midst of this compulsion to such dithering descant. He scans the ground for some one thing, for anything, for just enough, but still he comes up empty; he finds only some sunny day no longer in the present...that is no longer present but...that *this* now is encumbered, nay, *encompassed* by *in toto*, a peon to some vacant—yet vestigial—ideal...

φ

And so he thinks he understands the rule of such dissemblance, the organon by which appearance manifests as real—that set behind the landscape is what's set within the landscape; that the essence of the sighted is what's cobbled into view. What more could he depend upon to move... to move on *from*, he asks himself, but there's no answer, neither question to direct his affectation of a counterclaim. Too much more, he thinks, though even that without conviction, lacking any method to mark progress *or* decline...

φ

He's thinking too much more than this, than any just as this is, in *this* case what elicits his return to nearer stall; so the trick of superfluity that draws him to his nature was uttered into purpose by the maundering remains of some expectancy obstructed, a game of locks made level by the push and pull of tides. He that ever...ever...He that ever needs return to what returned him to his hope of second chances soon excoriates the cureless wound of certainty...

φ

What seems to him so hopeful — an *abundance* of resilience — is that he felt not only such a certainty when finding himself purposed into similar occasions in the past, but that the one he now recalls is still unusual in *some* way — still offers him a pretext for its unrivaled propinquity within his recollections, its character fit to the plight that sets his weary frame. Finally, a reason. Finally, *a cause*. He's sure that this peculiar apparatus, if it is in fact peculiar, he knows that he can't know...that this *control* he judges so specific in its nature is not only instrumental in the forming of his faculties, but also the appraisal of his place and fortune now. What he knows or *thinks* he knows...

φ

What he thinks he has *discovered* is the means by which some enterprise he roughly calls *conatus* chooses one form to return to over others that don't differ much in substance — in trace of shape or substance — despite its apposition to this or that occasion that's occasioned its recall. As if aptness were a quantity...were conceived as quantifiable...

φ

But it isn't, he assures himself, and that's the fitting point. What arrives as a constitutive reprise of this incipience —

what's *perfectly* understandable when considered from this stance—has failed to take account of both the practice and economy of such unwitting paragons, to understand the mechanism by which the shared coherence of the senses feigns the modal iterations of such egoless consent. What he thinks he has discovered—has *achieved*, devoid of want—is that the image is made flesh by an *associative* praxis, that within every presentiment lies a fleeting collocation to the seer—the *receptor*—without which no duration would be possible, so no seity assume appropriation *to pursuit*...

φ

Absent such duration—thus the buttress of enduring—one could never think the world as true, which is to say *as extant*. To say the truth *or* sense it, which he's sure are the same thing. That he may not be right is of no consequence; if he's wrong but it won't vary the trajectory of his *next* resolve, then it's not worth the working out until the future hits upon the means to sight that errant turn. As if that's stopped him elsewhere, but...

φ

Back to the point. He must go back to the point. Always back. He must always go back to the point. The point at which he started when he started to go back to the point, there on the bench beside the bounding benchside...

φ

He's departed from the point by recollecting his penultimate attempt to go back to the point—the last that he can *at this point* recall, if nothing more. And *that*, he recollects, was just the point of recollecting the return he *last* encountered;

he can't confirm, that is to say, that what he's named as last is in all actuality his lattermost attempt to make his way across the damascene of upland drifts and plaited groves, and this seems an imprudent gap in his sweep of awareness, a hint of what he torpidly bemoans his baneful ignorance, his flaccid grasp. He tells himself again it's inconceivable to *try* to tell oneself and find one's effort fallen short, that one could never fittingly identify a difference—chart some method *to distinguish*—between such failed attempts and those same acts of telling, of repeating as though telling...

φ

He tries to convince himself—one tries to convince oneself, he thinks—and this sort of endeavor is surely destined to be foiled, if you're made up...if you're *constituted* as he is, which is to say you test the claims of proffered propositions by confirming *to the world* the truth of propositions tested...

φ

It's the noteworthy impertinence of all such vain mimesis that *to try* is only meaningfully distinguished from *to do* if it's conceivable that one should try and fail. To say that one is trying to continue in the absence of some menace to that diffident assent—or some *imagined* menace, if nothing quite so fecund, quite so *real*—is as much of an absurdity as any vain tautology propounded as a premise, or a proof...

φ

It's ludicrous, he thinks, to think of trying to think, but to try to think of something...of *something else* when what one thinks of now commands attendant animus, and the thinking of the thinking otherwise—the *trying* to think otherwise—includes within its eidolon the thinking of the same, well, he thinks it needless to say—that it's demonstrably the case, that is, whether one actually does so... one thinks one *needs* to do so or not—that such attempts at focus often fail...

φ

And so he's reached his first conclusion—or if it's not his first, it's surely his *most recent*—that all attempts to tell *oneself* attempt to vouch for what one tells by means one knows are spurious, sometimes by appeal to an erratic inclination, and others the compulsive repetition of the same...

φ

Thus he tells himself; one only tries to tell oneself what one considers suspect...only *represents* oneself as trying to tell oneself after realizing that such attempt has failed. It is rare enough indeed, he tries to tell himself at present, to think that one is trying to tell oneself at present, meaning what one tells oneself right now one knows is wrong...

φ

That the last time he took foot into the thatch was the last the sun unfurled its rosy fingers through the slack of cumulous shroud, or that the last sun at his back was the last time that the sun was at his back—the last that he could *taste the gleam* of sun against his back—seems so markedly implausible that he can't even tempt himself to ask for such a proof. What's more, he doesn't know why he should care or think it matters, or why he has claimed otherwise when he knows the claim is false...

φ

It's the last he can recall, which seems a reason to recall it, so why the first...the last avowal of its status as the first or last it happened? Why the yearning to make sequence in duration mirror order in the throb of his mnemonic throes? What reason for this puerile rage against such glib narration? For making of such wayward dreams a cipherable code? What reason to seek reason...

φ

It's not that what he now recalls was neither first nor last to meet the passing standard he considers its assemblage *at this instant*—its relevance to resources ready to hand— or that he's happened onto such a paltry sense of certitude by palpating what's in it, intrinsic to his recollection of that whilom trail, but that without some grasp of what enticed that single scrap from an infinity of remnants—of similars cast off into dissent, into *delay*—he can't be sure of its veracity—of its *significance*; that deprived of any motive to believe it worth remembering when others were not similarly sanctioned with a place within his ceaseless seriatim of a cryptic fray he doesn't know he's lived it, that he didn't simply *make it up* from random, disparate fragments, as an endless game...

φ

If so many of the world's best known occurrences can drift into the abject anonymity of absence—the silence of a history in common, and in common lost—then why should the remembrance of the lone, distracted quidnunc have to meet a greater canon, to justify its load as some variety of response? Why is it a problem that he recalls only one moment—whether of that fulgent piquancy or the crisis of some inner bloat—when so much of what's happened on the stage and scale of history—so much of what is *happening right now*, behind his back—has been forgotten without wherefore or demonstrable effect? When so much that is happening this instant goes unnoticed? Exempted from all practicable memory, or trace...

φ

There's a difference, he's concluded, or so he tells himself at least. The world stage he inhabits may be girded by the cosmos, but its modus—its *existence*—is still verified by sense. Such claim claims no reliance on some postural receptor; it may induce a unity of faculties entranced, but it still outstrips all deference to the charge of the extrinsic by apprehending sense as an accession to the compass of the sensor, a subjugated precinct that one's faculties acquit. This is only to suggest that what so many take as license to speak freely—even of the history of histories, perhaps— is not so different from *his* privilege, in that both require reason, not to think the past as extant but to unconceal the grounds on which that portion has been poised as a totality, a *fixed* result. Such singular prepotency is what in any order of causation serves to supplicate the past life of the seity who's lived it to the ends that selfsame seity occasions as the one life of the aggregate—of the surface, or the null of place...

φ

Why not, he has asked often enough...he asks himself *right now* of far greater import...Why not first invert this common folderol of latencies if only for a look at his surrender to surrender—a submission to completion and to task? Why not take the vital force that every *nous* is given and subject the apprehension that contrives it as duration to the same unyielding standards? Take the prospects and conditions that project the *I* as singular for the basis of discernment, the foreground of one's forthcoming arrival...

φ

He knows that there are things to which he pays no heed at present—at any present presently regarded as received— things whose very nature is to vanish without notice, to blunder by as though they've never happened in the first place *or* the last. And so within one's field of view, one's circumscribing bracket—the scene one can't preclude, that is, whatever one's restraint—one can always ascertain too many traits and idle facets, too many...

φ

Too many leaves and stones and grazing cracks upon pave-ment, too many extricated swathes of rot across the turf; too many turns of concrete trowels and puckered interstices, too many bits of crumbled rime and assymetric slough; too many sweeping swirls of air against one's shirt and trou-sers, too many languid gusts of rancid breath against one's skin; too many nerves, too many sighs, too many moments in each sigh...too many things that there are still too many of to name...

φ

The point is, he recalls, as though he's ever lost it, and perhaps he has...Perhaps he lost the point before he ever thought of pointing, of pointing to the pointer, sighting the reciter...

φ

If he's lost sight of the point, he thinks, perhaps he's never had the *second* sight to think of one such as his target — of any *one* point as his goal. As though an arbitrary aggregate of features — a convocation of distinctions brought together by proximity — makes the sign what it refers to, what refers it...

φ

The point is that there's something...some dull faculty, perhaps...that there's something that can pointedly account for *any* predicate, whether given as a trace effect of facultative sovereignty or the address of all claims to such ingenuous receipt — the simplest form of relevance contrived as comprehensible...as *comprehended* in the gamut of one's push to act. There must be some way of accounting for what's noticed, thereby counted; any counting that can be likewise accounted a descriptor — a *descriptive affectation* — of the merely real...

φ

One must justify one's choices, even if they're never chosen; one must seek some sense and purpose in the labor of omission — the act that sets the frontier of the limit, of the whole. In this sense, he thinks...Is it a sense? He's still uncertain, but that's never been a bar to his continuing...his ongoing *continuance* before...

φ

In this respect awareness of what's missing — what's *excluded* — from the last unknowing radius but that given second thought...given *enough time* for second thought appears a desultory aggregate of properties and predicates, reveals that there's a mechanism fixed within propinquity—the means by which one *brackets out* what's outside of one's bracket, and thereby gathers only and so much as one regards...

φ

One means only and so much, he thinks, everyone means only and so much—and nothing more. What is not *in* is ascertained the limit of the inner that the out excludes—the *inside* of the out, devised an outwardly enciphered scale—but what agitates him here is that so much is gone forever, without the chance to undertake recovery down the line; so much that can't be understood as having been, as *disappeared*, and so cannot be found...

φ

A tragedy, he thinks, of chance delays and bygone chances, and forthwith thinking of them he comes close enough to weeping to look down...to turn his eyes down towards the molder and reach up towards his lineaments. He anticipates his tears, that is, and readying himself for what's most usually demanded after such leakage transpires he draws his arm up towards his eye, his left arm, as it chances, and so the sleeves that swathe it, the sleeve of blouse beneath the sleeve of jacket, it goes without saying, without wanting or saying, without either wanting to move what moves with what one wants to move or saying what moves with what one wants to move, which self-evidently...which *it goes without saying* has nothing to do with whether such a saying happens, whether *thinking of* such saying ever happens...

φ

And so he lifts the left arm and the sleeves that swell around it, and so the skin and gore and bone beneath them to his eye—his left eye, as it turns out, he's chosen that arm for a reason—the eye which holds a fullness he associates with…with absence, he recalls—the sudden realization that some unwitting elision can't be rectified by any future strain. He lifts the sleeves up to the eye—left to left, he fancies—while pulling right arm into torso, and stretching both eyes wide…

φ

It's difficult to lift the lids discretely for the purpose—the purpose of the opening such alluvium requires. He realizes the raising of the right lid seems superfluous, but only with respect to the peculiar task at hand. It may serve any of a myriad of purposes not coincident with the effect the dilation of the left means to enjoin—to assist him, for example, in the keeping of his balance while he reaches for the discharge…

φ

He moves to wipe the grimy sleeves across his gaping oculus, stretched wide as if a snake's mouth fit to swallow up the sky. He thinks of all that's missing, all that's left of all that's missing, so to conjure what the movement of his arm hopes to belay. It's such a waste, he thinks, such a waste of time and effort, attempting to dissemble what is yet a *nearing* anguish, a bereavement that's predicted but that's never come to pass. Such a waste. As if the proper use of anything can be presumed his method in anything, for *any* aim or purpose. As if, that is, an inner loss were granted pride of precedence above the falling outside of the outside world...

φ

And so he draws his left arm to his excavated canthus, hoping that such apathy will mask what he *imagines* is still nearing its ebullience, to trickle cheek to jowl before it leaps to lower ground. It's not that he believes the interlopers who have taken up his harbor can now see him... have *ever* seen him, nor does he imagine they possess an interest in what interests his appearance of concern. He thinks, rather, that somewhere—perhaps beneath the hedges at the next turn in the byway—there are those who mean to find some inner defect in his carapace, his baggy verge; to tap the mourner's impulse that's advanced him to this fateful brink, this null of huddled dreams and *supplantations*...

φ

Yes, he has a fate he hopes to tease out from its passage, a fate he'd like to witness...to *establish*—then replace. Replace with what, one might well ask, but that does not dissuade him; it may be but an image of privation—of an affable *impasse*—but this remains sufficient to foment his next arousal, so to add the feint of rhythm to his languid dance...

φ

He lifts the grimy cloth that sheathes the left arm towards his vizard, he opens wide his blinkers to reveal the cloudy sky, he hopes to wipe the tears away, the tears that haven't come yet, the tears that haven't come, that aren't coming... The tears that aren't coming aren't failing to come fast enough to stop him from releasing arm up to his tearless eye,

37

and so what had been clear but for the vague vaticination of effusions still gone missing is confronted—is *invaded*—by a far more toxic tonic, the shit up to the elbow that serves him as array. What searing pain, what bracing indignation fills his senses! He rears against the force of this reminder...this *remainder* of a world beneath, a world behind—the world that fills his clothes...

φ

It's just this breed of cark, he thinks, this *species* of infraction—the shock of what must *always* remain novel, what can never shake the sheen that shrouds the new—that led him to this tumult...to this *bother* to begin with; it's just this sort of novelty that's brought him to his insight, his knowledge of what's absent from his knowledge of what's absent...of what's missing from his sense of all that's missing from...He has, he thinks, revealed some part...some something about some part *of* himself *to* himself—a pose he was not only unaware of before this one, but that he did not for a moment have the impulse to inhabit, or suspect...

φ

Thinking that he never once suspected the putrescence of his raiment—of what now *substitutes* for raiment—says nothing of his having had some cause for the suspicion in the past. He thinks that if he'd thought about it even for an instant he would surely have determined what has since become quite plain—that he's as noisome as is possible for such a host to provender, that no more filth can ever braze its seething hash to him...

φ

more, to here describe the trouble of delaying such description — to give to every impulse the impulsive sweep of scale that such mimesis makes imperative, as a range implied — but he simply can't envisage any means to reach that causatum without indulging in a similar elision of the process of elision...

φ

And so he's had to make due with another explanation... another *form* of explanation he thinks good enough for now. He presently has settled on what he's only just now settled on, a truism as true of any iterative plaint — of every other artifice made subject to the same deferred mechanics of design. He has, again, reverted to assertion for his start point, a point he may repudiate, but without distinct effect...A point he'd rather *not* concede, that he'd as soon oppugn but for the contrary conviction that he's never had a choice. A point...a point of order, or...

φ

In order to make sense of his peculiar inclinations — and how, that is, they travel from conception into act — he knows he must begin...he must *have already begun* from some mark never once imagined in his clamber towards fulfillment, acknowledging such principles have not met his native wont. In acting towards some end, he thinks, however vague one's purpose — what entices one to thinking it's the *thing to do* — one must practice an elision not contrived as either practice *or* a practice that's elided; one must practice before practice becomes possible, thus elide the practice of elision he is hoping now to represent as practice, knowing that in consequence all such reverie is vanquished, that he's got it wrong again. He *understands*, that is to say, that every act of understanding leaves behind what's lacking or superfluous to its specific...its *determined* ends, whatever they may prove, or prove against...

φ

Alas, even *this* point—this torpid *stab* at explanation—distracts him from the question he began...he began this explanation *with*, another indigestible consumption he feels certain has confronted him at some pass before this one, but to no purpose he recalls in taking up this pitch. Thus the problem of prognosis that needs neither the capacity to limn its mode in full—the method that invigorates one's portion towards some...towards *any* aim at all—nor holds within that predicable promise the surrendering of reason to the limning of the limning of such erratic focus, of such nebulous regard...

φ

In the opening of vision—the coming into view—that makes intrinsic one's presumptive impetus of an aim, one must avoid the thinking...the *awareness* of each turn that serves to manumit that finish; one must apprehend, that is—and by such idle means construe—an ordering of predicates that needs some steadfast effort to take form. And how make that distinction in the species of one's making of distinctions? How draw that declension of a typos from its undiscovered substance into *plein air*, into...

φ

Well, he thinks in fleeting supplication to his purpose—to what he thinks will someday represent his purpose, to *specify* the reflex he's determined is the substance of his motive force in full—there is a sort of clue set up within the world prepared...the word by which he's predisposed his telling of a world prepared for action, a world at once begotten to describe as his abode. In every act accomplished—that has met its consummation as a *patent* end—one must first understand...*have understood* the structure that endows some *ad hoc* transit with amazement, as an *unexpected* stage; the judgment that, unheralded, would surely have resulted in distraction from said purpose, or the failure of all movement towards such paramount resolve. Within every collusion of desire and experiment—whatever its residuum, what such an easy unity of principle forebodes—one can't help but identify conditions absent which the failure of that craved potentiality is certain, conditions of pursuit that will not happen without effort on the part of that whose concept of an outcome...of *velleity* in service to an outcome reveals those disparate amplitudes as once again a whole. Again, he thinks, again again he thinks...

φ

He thinks it strange enough that every juncture of transition between premises—what he assumes will soon appear as premises *affirmed*—must come upon him in some situation and no other...no other than the substance of that coming to the fore. He thinks it both distracting and without justification...*distractingly unjustified* that he should feel within himself such easy resolution...should feel it in some instant in particular, that is, that it should ever have to be... has ever *been* corporeal...

φ

It is the pose of singularity—of *being singular*, he thinks; it is his singularity that he judges most unnerving, the sense he has that he's becoming singularly disparate in his affects and deceptions, the very same distraction that distracts him...that distracts him at the moment...

φ

What designates an action—even one of interruption—as a *singular* prepotency, what makes even the most fulfilled diversion from one's chosen course seem nonetheless a whole, is that in bringing it to happenstance—in *making it happen*—one must have thought of every bound that's capable of ending the dominion of that purpose in particular; the fulfillment of the function its protagonist prefigures, then compels...

φ

The substance of one's know-how comes in knowing how to journey down the path towards the fulfillment of one's prepossessing goals, thus *proving* one knows how amounts to making something happen at one's whimsy, on command. In order to know how, that is—to prove one's skill *ostensive*—one must conjure the repeatable coincidence of wants with their imagined satisfactions; one must meet the expiation of one's chosen ends precisely when one chooses them...

φ

One might induce desired ends by any means or measure, and if the action is repeatable—if one can offer up the spectacle of metamorphosis again—then such hermetic affect will be granted the esteem of confirmation, the catalyst of demonstrated ken. There's nothing more required of such base epistemology than that some situation comes

be so bad at all...

φ

Why try to avoid what cannot be avoided, what in the end
is sure to be the end of all attempts? Delaying the decided
can be justified—can be *reasonable*; there are surely times
when even the most urgent of injunctions can be put off to
another day, another stance—for just as long as possible,
presuming its relent—and others when one might assume
it best to get it over with, but in any case the choice—the
knowing *how* to choose that leads one closer to result—is
always better proffered than its obverse—the act of giving
in to what amounts to chance...

φ

In *this* case, he believes...He believes that if he could now
come to understand his circumstance—the particular palaver he's been stuck in from the start—as a case...a case *in
point*, then he might find...might be able to *decide* a way to
clear it, one of many stratagems he's sure he must...he *will*
endure, all in good time...

φ

He's not only slumped at midriff in reaction to the reek-
ing clutch of apathetic sleeves—an apathy, he well recalls,
towards which his further...his most *recent* parley is addressed, if not received—but just beyond that inverse pose
awaits the loss of his estate within the lurid vistas of his
jejune reminiscence, a portent of his forthcoming...his *inev-
itable* encounter with the ouster—what tallies up, he reck-
ons, to the boundless *set* of ousters—that heretofore have
taken up his brothel as a bunk. Or the opposite. That occupy

his purview as a haven, his harbor as a whore's bed or a pimp's turf...

φ

He is, he thinks, in such a fell and crudely fraught predic-ament—in mind and body both, with neither prospect nor recourse—that his only chance at solving any one of the con-ditions that make up his immurement lies in solving every one, perhaps in series...He identifies his hope, that is, in viewing this predicament as many but still one, all follow-ing from cornerstone to apex in a blink. He must begin con-struction, the construction of the ruin his life amounts to...

φ

He must *understand* the makeup of the life his ruin amounts to, a chiastic approbation that has suddenly emerged, notwithstanding the enjoyment he—*anyone*, really— would be inclined to muster in response to its odd form. That said—such reduction to this thickened broth of fun-daments *put off*—he knows that *this* time he has come to *this* place, a world turned upside down...and downside...

φ

The measure of the sooth of such imperious rhetoricals—the rhetorical opposition between two such fecund modes—is that when placed into that saltatory binary of predicates the absence of the one implies the presence of the other—the measure of the facing of the one is the backing of the other— each required by the sentiment construed to fit its pairing, its completion in the pertinence of the whole. Every upside down is downside up, he thinks it's proven; up and down cannot both be thought down at the same point, for the prin-

know at this point, but he's begun to understand...*to try* to understand the method by which he has always formerly forgotten what he knows as of a piece with that deficient anamnesis which first forced him to remember the forgetting *that* he knows and *what* he knows as of a piece, as of the same protracting excess and impermeable stripe. Would that he could somehow think it otherwise...that anyone could ever think it otherwise, he thinks...Would that he could turn back to that time before the time he now inhabits to find something like...like *a vision* something like his own, if not precisely that, if like but still outside of...

φ

If one can be assured of always skipping over something, or having always left something behind...If one can make the case with an inviolable authority that something's always *gone off* the corruption, spoiled the perfection—the *perfect putrefaction*—of one's mimetic faculties in practice and in kind—and he can, he has, he knows it still a far sight more distinctly...more *securely* than he knows his present place within this bulging vale...

φ

If one's certainty in coming to the prospect of one's certainty is understood a practice of occluding every method but the method of occlusion—of forgetting almost everything of all that's been perceived—then might one not quite rationally—again to say *repeatably*—dispute some claimed awareness made a subject...*subjected to* that culling of propinquitous delays? Why is it a problem to believe what one remembers—what *constitutes* one's chance attempts to gather in the moil—should one day be suborned again to some presumptive standard, allowing one to think that *future* episode as actual, thus *saved*...

φ

Saved, yea, it's his longing to be salvaged from the scrap heap of mimesis, the constitution of the fête he's occupying now. He surmises something new, he thinks, newer than he did before he understood the pivotal privation of his standing to begin with—the vestiges of processes that never will be named. He knows that he's had knowledge...that to know that he's had knowledge *he's forgotten* is to claim that knowing anything requires the elision of its outside, of what had first appeared its seamless whole; that knowing the immurements of his knowing, of his vision—the critical *system* of each collated stroke its indefatigable nil— presents the possibility of some secure foundation; *exemplifies*, that is, a kind of episteme immune to the putrescence of the fallow sward, the world outside...

φ

Every knowing has within it two modes of expression, two states held in contrast...that *oppose* by being both intrinsically exclusive and implying such exclusion from the obverse of its absent void. Knowing one one must know two—he thinks he's proved it soundly—and when each half of that coupling is ascertained as singular—as one of two, that is to say, or exclusively as one—the canny pundit finds its other present in its precinct, an infinite of binaries from which there's no escape. In two they are, they are in two, the two significations that are balanced as a proof— that which first is given by the *tromp l'oeil* of the senses, and that secondary vestige ever present as *noesis*, the eidetic purchase granted every prodigal result. The first presents as potency, the second as discernment, and each has its

on his way from this to that—he has not once, not even once, forgotten how to supplicate, or how keep withered bronchi gulping rancid gas...

φ

All to say it's *neither* an instinctual nor autonomic expertise he's after, acts that seem as much unwitting reflex as indentures to discernible intent. That's the difference, he conjectures, between character and craving—that any semblant humor of the typos thus enciphered is accordingly adept at its insensible achievements, in ferreting its substance, say, from earth and wood and rotting flesh...

φ

He finds no rationale to think that *every* flailing ego trapped in service to some stipulated leaning—some efficacious *sustenance* to which its tattered intellect resorts—is able to fulfill such aspiration with proficiency identical to that had by all others equally forsaken to a wallow in that coded lot. What's required is that every cunning specificity of the sort should first assuage its indeterminate requirements sufficiently—with a parallel...a *commensurate* sufficiency...

φ

What could it mean to postulate some one presumed sufficiency *more* sufficient than another? How achieve a finer shade within that fixed control? If one acquits oneself with added force of respiration, receiving greater volume of recuperative air with every miniscule persuasion of the pulmonary girth, would one think that one had somehow brought off breathing with a *greater than*, or set a higher bar for the deportment into gasp? An absurdity that indicates the means he means by such impassive approbation, by differing what *merely* is sufficient from its obverse—his directive to necessity...

φ

But that's not it at all, he thinks, employing his new prowess; he's willing to consolidate his burden...his *deduction* of a premise only recently relayed to prove that what opposes his necessity is *never* the sufficient, as there's nothing contradictory in thinking something both—in *being both*, that is to say, unmindful of one's stance. What opposes the sufficient is...he can think of nothing other than...of nothing yet an *other than*...

φ

A thing is either sufficient or not; there is no middle purchase. What's confusing him again—what's been confusing *from the start*—is that two acts can be correctly thought sufficient to divergent ends but still adduce an asymmetrical...an *opposing* propriety when considered as the means to some companionable thrust; that countless and entirely discrepant superficies are sufficient to forestall some one presentiment in particular and only some of them retain that imprimatur in relation to a contrary... to what *in this respect* appears a contrary result...

φ

Thus two different breathers—as though there's ever been some multiplicity of such construed *the same*—may readily maintain the nap of anaerobic function required to perdure through this one moment and so hit upon the next one... the next one next to this one, or the next one after that, but

the champion in respiratory exercise will be the sole protagonist endowed to the achievement of some feat of desperate vigor, some vigor that's sustained over the whole
length of the course...

φ

There is, in any case...*disregarding* what the nature of pursuance one subjects to such coarse assay, and with what great
advantage one effectuates its aims...there is always a distinction between such feckless praxis and the notion *he's*
refining, an idyll of the ideal that he hasn't yet discerned.
And even further...He's willing to go further; the driving force, he thinks, that plots the phenotype of instinct—
what's given as intrinsic skill, and not a studied art—only
slightly differs in its iterative aspect from the reflex, an
expertise developed without ever being taught...

φ

So the child ambulates with average growth and practice,
but it doesn't need the talent to be demonstrated first. The
wolf begins to hunt, the goat to graze, the crow to scavenge,
but in each instance the practice seems so near innate to its
exemplar—every sustenance maintained by that incalcula-
ble stroke—that for the purposes of this...of *all* taxonomies
of praxis it remains largely a model of instinctual pursuit.
Of unmediated drive, that is, and not just largely either;
wholly, he would like to say, not muttering a word...

φ

The foremost attribute of that form of acquaintance he's
forgotten...he's known and then forgotten—foremost in
his survey of the problem, or the problem *solved*—is that

such a forgetting would not terminate one's provender, while the faculty to harbor is another thing, another...

φ

What he's looking for, he thinks, is still a manner of proficiency peculiar to those beings...to those *knowers* who are capable of learning from *new* circumstance, whose inculcation of things known can be forgotten without necessary... without *pre*determined outcome or refractory result. It's a difficult distinction to make sense of—to reveal even the *means* to *get across*—despite his doing so so often that he can't conceive a limit to the catalogue of instances...

φ

What could it mean to codify...to *list out* all the figures of an infinite set? How compose a muster of such fixed instantiations not limited by number, but by secondary character or generalizing predicate? It is possible, he thinks, although the fact is strange enough...

φ

One can only understand—or make discernibly *distinct*—the notion of quantity in the first place if such finitude is not a limit on the concept of set—as long, that is, as fragmentary sums are as attainable as those one thinks compendious...those that one can picture as *complete*. And so there is motility inherent in the concept...every singular *conception* brought to meaning *more than once*; that insofar as everything that means presents as singular it's a member of a set without a limit—without limit to its aggregate; an amity whose membership would take an endless interval to list...

φ

It seems inconsequential that in consequence of such a superfluity of know-how he knows that he will never come to know the world *in toto*, that he'll never find a way to show...*to represent* what is eternally extending from this moment—from *every* moment—to the next one, and the next. He doesn't think it matters because...He doesn't know precisely why he doesn't think it matters; perhaps, he thinks, it's too soon to take action towards deferment— deferment to some more inclusive cull...

φ

He imagines, for example, that without such bold compulsion—such absence of imperative in furtherance of intent— it would be impossible to accomplish almost anything, meaning all that's still required of a seity as circumspect as his in his desire...in the *fulfillment* of his desire to construct a world both tacit and complete. Why, one would be lost in cerebration, one would never achieve anything but progress *towards* completion of a project that lies infinitely distant from its end. It makes him laugh, now that he thinks of it; now that he thinks of it he chuckles for a moment, which would matter very little, but...

φ

Which matters very little, insofar as it's a commonplace, to him as to so many who are of his rank and kind...Which would matter very little, if it weren't for his balance at the moment of the spasm, a posture which requires some great stillness—some great *concentration* of stillness—to maintain. This is all to say that finding humor in the prison of predicaments he's managed to avoid—predicaments *he thinks* he has avoided, if the premise isn't clear—has required him to change his pose of liminal inversion in the hope—which he still holds—of keeping torso from collision with the spoil at his footing, of withholding weary noggin from the bounding scourge…

φ

His desire to keep all but his extremities from grazing against anything but open air—anything *distinct from* his own corpulence extending mutely aft and through the sea of open air—is what obliges one foot from the burrow of its marker, a balance made unstable by that unforeseen convulsion from the core. He thinks it's not that funny, and he knows it to be true, but he is also convinced—a conviction drawn from so much repetition of the shudder he tolerates no avarice to think it out, to think it through—that this compulsion to display was scarcely worth it…was paid for with a shift of balance most assuredly *not* worth the paltry pleasure of the throe, and that this ludic pitch into awareness will be no effective tocsin against doing just the same the next time round…

φ

He knows the next time round will be no different, just as this one made no progress in affecting such steadfastness by its having been repeated countless times before. He speculates…he's *sure*, that is, he'll come to see a next time, and that he will go through it; that going through it once again will prove as fruitless and cantankerous as this dull iteration, now that he can plot it…has *endured it*…

φ

At least it won't last long, he thinks—a pittance of a privilege. No one could want more than the cessation of such suffering while in it. It hasn't lasted long, a state he's willing to attribute to a statement...an *activity* of inner will that manifests an outside by its stillness, by the stillness of the subject who suborns it...

φ

And perhaps this vague achievement—this resumption of control before his suffering abandon is objectified in consequence—can be made to seem ascendant by the loss of static balance, thus the meeting of his foretop with the fallow ground...Perhaps that he has managed to redeem his failing purchase in the past is due in large part to his many previous pursuits of such comportment, knowing as he does so that the jubilant initiative which started the convulsion must be quashed before the shaking stops. One must *stop being pleased*, stop finding pleasure, which is arduous enough in principle to discourage almost everyone who's been similarly satisfied from seeking its surcease. It's not that he can't feel it...can't feel the delectation; not that he's incapable of being thus bewitched, a state he presumes justified...he thinks *requires* nothing more than the prognosis of prostration to continue, to surrender it's impenitent perceiver to...

φ

He has oft enough been pleased to know that being pleased is pleasing; he'd rather be pleased than not, that is, an apothegm assumed by being thus deemed capable of any choice at all. To say that one is pleased, he thinks, portends one's preference to remain within that fervor, that one would only willingly conclude it for a joy that's at least *equal* in its measure, though more likely for a greater turn. One may be mistaken in one's anticipations, supposing what's around the bend will be apt compensation for the gainsay of some tractable malaise and have that supposition proven false—proven against—but in each case one who's able...*who is capable* of amusement will court that feeling state over all else...

φ

He does *not* think that one's exclusive purpose is in pleasure—pleasure for all purposes *derived* from other ends—but rather that one's pleasures and the meeting of one's motives with the greatest good conceived therein are only thought as manifest by looking back—by *retrospection*; that as they *happen* they are not apparently distinct...

φ

The failure of all bids to prove some egoistic rectitude the *conatus* of anything one might construe as *will* comes from the fact that such attempts prefer the same unquestioned bias as a comparably compelling, but exactly obverse claim; in both visions the indicated motive and its causatum are seen as some ideally formed divergence from the whole, a differentiation with its basis in the same order of evidence by which one thinks each term of the equation *without* difference, made one by the discernment of the subject to whom such categorical dissection of phenomena is given, and so *for* whom it's incidence...its passage *into* incidence is trained...

φ

What he means to argue is far less than what this posture

of inured signification—of dissembled clues—propounds; he does not mean to take on any practice or its unrequited counter, to bandy an adherence to a system of imperatives without which no one good could be attended, so confirmed. He does not want to here pursue the audit he's pursuing; it does not please him in the least, he wants to now move on. It's not that it's not interesting enough—and interest, he'll admit, is a pleasure he's most usually reluctant to relinquish—but it's merely *being interesting* suggests a lesser pleasure than he expects in the pursuit of something more...

φ

And it's even worse. He doesn't only represent...*expect* a situation closer to his liking to come lunging into presence should he manage to forgo what seems to draw his focus hence, nor believe that such pretension would cause something else to happen, something painful he'd avoid if he could but keep up his stance. He does both, believes at *both* ends of this passage he will realize some clear benefit if he's able to forsake all further succor of such indigent reprisal... such reprise of certain indigence...

φ

In brief, he thinks, one only seeks that pleasure one can muster as an image from the prospect of the most expansive purview one can muster, a purview understood as sensibility or ground—the further the expansion, the more distantly related to an egoistic discipline...

φ

The closer he habituates his involuted focus to some median...some *purely* median horizon, the nearer drifts his longing towards an infinite abatement, the inertia of an infinite *resolve*. An economy of scale, he thinks, but still...

φ

His pleasure in the featureless coincidence of his own illimitable excursus having landed on the vision and the welter of illimitable excursus has not thereby resulted in reward for his small efforts towards resurgence, vindicating—as if it were his purpose—the pleasure he takes in thinking of that *telos* as an end in itself. His mania to stop from any further bow to stasis in the simpering deferment of his simpering resolve to make a move towards *recommencement* has nothing to do with an absence of a full appreciation of the moment...of the *pleasure* of the moment, but is another demonstration of compliance with what's happening in consequence of the drollery that's happening right now...

φ

It's not that he construes himself *opposed* to such behavior...such *expression* of a pleasure, when the urge hits him head on, but now, just at this moment, his inversion of the attitude most usually resulting from one's standing on the boulevard—his subtle derogation of all *proper* ease, all right repose—makes any further deference to that preternatural seizure seem a longing for the terminus the first sputter evoked, face flush with the rancid muck that covers his cadaver, no less than the adjacent mount...

φ

It can come as no surprise—it can read as no great *insight*—that when one can predict extended suffering in consequence of briefest joy one is likely to endeavor the avoidance of the pain over the experience of the pleasure; there are kindred choices made more difficult to predict by some comparative intensity—some difference in demonstrable *extent*—but this seems unimportant to the case as it presents itself...as he *conceives* it presently, if nothing more impressive, or more palpably corrupt...

φ

It should come as no surprise that he chooses...that he's *chosen* to remit his growing jouissance before his head hits mucilage of saturated loam, but that he's *able* to do so—that it's still within his power to halt this second iteration of his whelming joy at merely *thinking* his condition, to stop himself from any next convulsion by surrendering his vigor to a balance thereby anchored and secured—is more than any common skill or facultative longing, and so seems not an expertise *he'd* likely have achieved. He's satisfied, he thinks, he's even *pleased* with this ability to keep his carriage stable in defiance of the heartaches he's subjected himself to...he's *subjected to*, that is, without a need to cede the details to a purpose that's intrinsic—that's prospectively intrinsic—or *assumed*...

φ

He feels himself *accomplished*, flushed with surreptitious pride, while having no cause to deny such paltry enterprise a place within the purview of all others of his kind—of any other intellect he's understood as equal, if not by act then by design. That there are many willing to forgo this satisfaction is a fact he's well aware of—of which, that is, he counts himself conspicuously aware; he knows that some who are inclined to leverage such collateral are nonetheless so wildly impulsive in pursuit of greater joy that it's beyond their scant capacity to resist its vain attraction—for any reason any way at all...

φ

One might feel so enraptured by some, disport of the faculties that stopping it...that no effect is great enough to justify one's stopping it, no matter what its perquisites of misery or pain. Indeed, he thinks it plausible to think the obverse true—with respect to the experience of pain, to the *assize* of any momentary joy against the hardship brought upon by its remittance, its intractable deferral to...

φ

He speculates that if his balance falters for a moment he will find himself so far from any easement of his purpose that the progress he's made so far will be wasted, will be lost. In this sense, he believes, the pain that's creeping up behind him—the pain of losing all sense of his status in relation to his vacant range, his voided troth—is not so much a stimulus to any eager organ as it is an expectation of a labor without stop. He would be displeased, he would *find it painful*...

φ

He finds it painful to conceive of all he'd likely have to go through to return only to this point—to this point once again—should he casually relinquish what small gains he's managed so far, those gains he's thought to stipulate as legacy, as *his* demesne. He imagines the frustration of his having to rise up—to *lift himself up*—as though it were an insult, an offense against the effort he's embodied by this strain. His frustration at the endless repetition of the exploit of attaining such a meager state is considerably greater than the same plight first approached from the perspective of first notice, of one's *inaugural* submission to the pattern—to the *system*—as a newfound dream...

φ

That this peculiar episode is nonetheless *not* novel—that the fact that it's peculiar doesn't mean it hasn't happened in some erstwhile span—has not escaped him, nor would he expect his furtive auditors to fail to see this very state implied in his arrival at such swift resolve. His indefinite response, that is, to this discrete occasion is not at all peculiar to one who's come upon it even once before. Take, for example, his focus on a consequence accessible to anyone provisioned with such balance—who has taken on a stance of any stable sort at all—and notice that assumed by this reaction is a knowledge of the ends towards which that consequence propels him...*would* propel him should he fail to circumnavigate the mire by his present stall...

φ

There was a time before this, before this new concern, when falling down seemed no more than a nuisance, a state demanding only that one stand back up again. Easier said than done, he thinks in knowing resignation, knowing as he does so that this has never been his means...*within* his means to do or think, to think or...

φ

There are those, he's almost certain—a rhetorical expedient he's almost certain substitutes for proof—for whom the act of rising up...of *lifting oneself lengthwise* from the heave of lea or pavement requires neither skill nor measurable passage to acquit. It's not that he's seen many—that there's any single instance of such feat he has in mind—but to his amazement he believes it makes no difference; he's apparently still able to adopt this understanding of the state of his compatriots absent any further evidence, and for some uncertain logic this thought...this *complaint*, as he regards it, doesn't bother him at all...

φ

Every earthbound organon will recognize what falling down a precipice surmounted by the strife and strain of froward crawl amounts to, a tragedy of lost time and relentless disappointment that no able bodied gull need soon abjure. One imagines the frustrations one has had to *suffer through*, and so would need to brook again to manage a return; the impediment of the first step, the toxic ooze of long ago excoriated sockets, the plod of spasms far too often thwarted to be gains; that there's no guarantee that one will dodge the same aggrievements the next time one sets sight upon the summit, and...

φ

And how has he surmised his plight a parallel scenario? How can he believe himself contrived to meet such forecast when he has...when he *possesses* all his pieces, all his members, fit to form? Well, funny you should ask, he thinks, addressing his own person; funny that this present scene should bring him back to intervals made real by implication but that he can't remember *in extenso*, as a designated mode. He is flooded with so many like ideas and speculations—so many intromittent thoughts and tocsins against

80

fate—that it's no surprise to him most will adduce as titil-
lations, are arrived at by osmosis; that the way he comes to
comprehend the new when he confronts it is by filing away
the sensitivity of viscera thus ingressed, not by sighting the
extrinsic goad that triggers such response...

φ

He knows that he recalls only so much of his experience,
and in answer to that tragic loss—that epiphany the same—
the sense of shrill foreboding...the shrill sense of foreboding serves him as a method—as an autonomic skillset—by
which to keep his waking mind uncluttered, and so clean.
It often doesn't work, he thinks, it doesn't work that often;
it works for what it must, but no sight further...

φ

Which is to say that if he'd found it requisite to recollect
what's happened in some...in *any* sort of detail—transfigured into litany whenever he'd attempted to push forward in avoidance of the next decline—then it would never
happen in enough time to allow for a reaction, a *kinesis*; to
quicken at the moment that the danger makes its presence
felt, no matter what the skill of his mimetic feats in turn.
The feeling gives him impetus—accelerates him forward,
as a force opposed—even as his wont is to give voice to its
description, an epilogue he knows he can't project before
he's settled—before he's found a way to some next finding
of a way to move along...

φ

That the spasm was itself a kind of action without acting—an
expression of an inner state that's equal to enduring it—has

not fully eluded his bestowal of attention, in defiance of his need to look away. His *yearning*, more exactly, although he won't admit it. He won't *confess* desire to exempt such ribald slogging from the scrutiny by which he's most inclined to meet the spectacle with passive faith, as some lethargic lizard scans the crepuscule for hints of morning light. He wants to look away, or rather, he *wanted* to do so, it was his only choice when first the paroxysm hit, and now...now that it's over...that it's come to fitting ease within some pulmonary abscess, he can at last survey the course by which the breakdown happened — or he can try to, he concedes, acknowledging he'll fail...

φ

He would revel in recalling the events as they occurred, but this time without deference...without deference or deferral to what's generally thought causative, the incidental leaning of the world that brought it on — the world for which the act acts as memento, scans as vestige; the last and first acceptance of the insight now it's...

φ

He would like to bypass any further assay of the antic, of the ferment that concussed him nearly off his level heels, and instead turn his attention to the feeling brought about by that coincidence of features, an affect he can't justify distinguishing from its expression — from the idiom of feeling at the moment it was...

φ

It is this *verity*, he thinks, that serves to differ such crude voicings of impermeable viscera from those affective states only by capable conviction made to open up as fully to an open world, and so he thinks this proxy for persuasion the first measure of what separates the episode from those stints of emotive truck he still believes the same. Different from the same by being same where same is different, by seeming an identical where all others are made same by force of differentiation...

φ

What other meaning impulse can claim such equivocation... such equivocal *locution*, as a latent field? Is some undetermined sadness—some mere *consciousness* of anguish—so far from its expression? Doesn't keening come as quickly after its inceptive goad? He's sure he has control over his affects as they slither over supplicating countenance, and while that may say little—perhaps nothing—about what draws him towards his ruling goal—nothing of the nature of that choler as a cerement of penury or providence, of things as they are entered in the present fold—it seems to be enough for him to concentrate on what alone concerns him at the moment; that feeling of subsistence—of identity as substance—he can't differ from its quantum, its embodiment as semblance, as dissembled guise...

φ

But there's something about laughter—the *experience* of laughter—that shares common cause with all that aforementioned plodding forward, only in direct relation to one's ego as an active gorm. It is not that it inscribes a generalized necessity, nor that he can't control it just as he controls his breath, but that controlling such a frenzy must in turn control the stretch that frames that voicing as an inner state. So does such expression disclose one of many poses of the feeling it expresses, and not an act that differs in its ration or its mode; it renders as a mode, that is, an aspect of the focal glut it also makes apparent, by which he means fulfillment of the state that it expresses, without which there would be no way to feel its force in full...

φ

There are some modes of existence whose *disclosure* is a species of awareness, a predicate distinguished from the whole in which it plays some trifling part. Contrasting the particularity of such mirthful paroxysm with the state of resignation that endures that discomposure doesn't mean that the relation between elements is causal, and it's this predisposition to think everything by reference to some undiscovered motive that makes false associations of such disparate parts...

φ

Wholeness, as he thinks it—*unity*, better still—does not preclude the stutter step of differentiation, even when it's set within the frame of singularity to which that inferential claim of unity refers. Is it not the mode that makes of any ideation a precursor to knowledge fitly geared or trespassed soon? Is not all conjectured as noetic made available...made *possible* by finding in the figure an infinity of deferments, and within that same assemblage the sameness of some single whole? The sameness of the selfsame, of the difference...

φ

Yes, it is a principle of ordinal intellection that can hardly be surrendered—that can never be *displaced*—but he would like to keep himself from making too much of the point. One must choose one's battles, or rather—and for the same reason—one must choose one's standing posture as one presses ever forward, without undue attention to the feelings of the vanquished or the interest of those patrons who take pillage for a sport. He would like to now move on, he thinks, or move back, in distinction...

φ

He would like to now move back to what he's moved on towards, a subtlety of purpose even *he* can't make less clear. That his whist and fleet analysis of such brutish cachinnation has only led him slantwise, without a way back to the assay that impelled him to *this* pose, is exactly the diversion that's led back to the assay that impelled him to diversion...

φ

There are things one does unwittingly—*unwillingly*, perhaps; things one finds compelling as a matter of course, but such determinations are not what one calls know-how, even if when ceded to some vacant thinking *of* them one can claim without duplicity that one knows *how* to do them, for knowing how to block their course, as surely and as quick. One knows that one knows how to breathe by willing its restraint, how to make one's heart beat faster only if with equal skill one can induce its rest. And even though he's certain all his organs pump and glisten, that his processes continue in the midst of his collapse, his viscera remains largely beyond any attempts he's made to function *less*...

φ

So the eager adept who sees mind and body separate along

the inner bourne drawn out by what gives voice to will confuses aspect for substantive, the sanctity of modus for the nonpareil of form. Just as the expression of emotive states seems foreign to their center—to their *character* as middle, or their circumstantial core—when considered from the aspect of the outside, from the inside they're but sight lines to the same ostensive landscape, an unremitting reflex to the almost whole...

φ

Somehow there's a way of knowing *knowing* that distinguishes such autonomic mastery of limits from those antecedent choices so absorbed into one's stirrings they resemble preconditions for the world in which such vagrant whims collide. Somehow the procedure by which he's learned his way around his mire makes that grasp appear intrinsic to his nature for as long as he refuses to recall a time before he first set foot within its bounds. Somehow it has bounds, he thinks, as clear as barbed-wire fences, a clarity that's only ever signed by the discomfort he betrays when he's approached, when he draws nigh...

φ

He knows when he approaches certain quarters he's uneasy—a feeling that prevents him moving feet first through the bar. It's not so much he wants to...that he wants to amble forward, not so much his need to—in an unknown land—explore, but rather to account for how he's come to this deportment—this most common of compulsive iterations on the mall—while still having no notion of its nature, of its *leaning*; of how he might suborn it to a latitude...

φ

He knows he's come to think the world in this...*through* this dire bearing; that if he simply moved on to a dream of new horizons the contours of the landscape would be comparably familiar and accordingly disgorged into the whole he finds so easy to map out with his intrusions—the project of his simpering carouse. There is a designated whole that he inscribes by *living in it*, by wearying its slipshod ruts and margins with his gate; a whole that he positions himself *on* as though a pedestal, as the baseline of his thinking without thinking it a thought. A constant he is only made aware of when it changes...

φ

He knows that there are those paths that reach well beyond his purview, paths that are accessible should he attempt to access them, to know them as he knows those paths he knows...He knows that all he's figured unfamiliar would become so—would in short order release to his concordance of a common view—should he only find the fortitude to take aim towards...

φ

Alas, when it comes down to it, whatever it, wherever up... when it's all said and done, that is, he really doesn't care about expanding his dominion, about making his world larger, or his options more diverse; what he has—what he's *been given*—has always been sufficient to release him from the longing for a bigger trough. What seems to him important in this otherwise resultless...this *futile* divagation is that somehow the existence of a world he doesn't know yet—a world he hasn't come across, for all his witless prods—suggests there may have been a time when this world as he knows it held the same elusive station; when even *this* world wasn't granted the esteem of being palpable, *or real*...

φ

It's not that such presumption is unreasonable...is *unreasoned* that disturbs him—that makes it so discomfiting, so shameful, as a lack—but that the image has no referent, and he simply can't recall a time when *this* world as it happens wasn't wholly in his grasp. And though this doesn't mean that he believes he's always been here—he has some vague recall of knowing nothing of this place—the extension... the *extrapolation* of the principle by which the world—*any* world, that is to say, without consideration of its lingering expanse—presents what seems a regress without...before... without before...without *against*...

φ

An out without which he can't understand his foundling nature, marshalled to the toxic bog on which his life's been limned; before asserting such familiarity with elsewhere... with what he can envision...what he *has*, that is, by no more than his fractional receipt of this collection of surveyed details. A world without an outside to make what's *in* preferred, without even the most obtuse conation towards preferment...

φ

What could it mean to think some world forgotten absent evidence of it's ever being known? Omission, true enough, is not the equal of forgetting; if something can't be brought to mind in the first place, then to postulate its absence in the second as a *separate* act is obviously wrong. There are, he knows, many species of remembrance, as the analysis to this reverse must certainly suggest. His thought is that somehow the very form of anamnesis that's routinely called remembrance is only really possible succeeding the construction of the ego in whose name such acts of disassociation—the dissociative shift from what is present here and now—are made to happen...are *completed*, regardless of the notice such an ego pays to sooth. There is something that connects the *actuality* of consciousness to recall, to *similitude*—any figure not at once distinguished by cessation...

φ

He likes to think that *everyone* was extant before being... before being *as* the self whose being is what they've become. He likes to think that he's at least in *this* way never singular, that somehow he can think of we and mean more than some *one*. And not *just* mean, but somehow *proffer* as a referent in the world for that mute commonweal, to think within his thoughts an actuality assured. When he thinks we, he thinks—and he does not do so often—he thinks that he is thinking not of others who might come to be as he is, as a rule, instead of those conjectured as coeval, as his *colleagues*, a fellowship contrived as parallel...

φ

He does not *know* if such persons are actual—or are, that is, concurrent with his thinking of them so; he does not have an inkling if they've dropped in on his inklings, and in any case does not have inclination to suppose. What he *does* know—what makes it possible for him to shake this subterfuge of level ground, of common trove—is that he's more than capable of thinking such plurality of purpose, or such *singular* purpose—such singular *existence*—held in plural, as a modal screed, and not only is he capable, he does so, he can't help it; that's precisely what he has and what he will...

φ

We've all had lives, he tells himself, before our having lived them—before one ever thinks oneself imbued with such *extent*. One may boast recollections of that primitive awakening but one cannot remember them; they are not collated to the threshold of one's being *as*, but settle as contortions of one's nature in pursuit. And so he wonders—how can one discern that passing debit to an absent past as substance...as the substance of the ego who can't otherwise identify a referent in the midst of that abstraction, that *distraint*? How conceive detection of a world *before* the presence of a seity to live it, to *receive* it, a seity that's presupposed condition for all intuitive...all *intuitional* convergence in the name of such receipt? And if it's not a concept, if it's *more* than a conception...

φ

If once he was a muling glob of viscid putrefaction—and it seems an easy inference from others of his kind—it was a time in his life—in the ontogeny of his corpus—that serves as precondition for the coming into being of the ego he lives now. That each such iteration of a solvency debased is likewise singular—is incapable of being interchanged—may not prove unexpected, but that doesn't mean he's found a way...but *he* still hasn't found a way...he thinks that no one's *ever* found a way to make that *mean* mean something...mean *anything* particular to this particularity,

90

this lived simultaneity of disparate voids...

φ

If one has come to being — come to *stasis*, in the flux — by virtue of reception...of the world held in receipt, then there must be a phase in the consumption of that moil that amounts to one's *receiving it* before one can construe the pose as aspect, or proclivity — before there is an I to eye that measureless extent. Why not, he thinks, fair enough; there are many things...many subtleties of his *own* juvenescence which he knows he has no prospect of recalling, and the fact does not concern him in the least. He's not concerned, that is to say, he has not been thus far and will not change his inclination, not without some benefice of the changing made apparent...made *demonstrable*, as a known effect. Of turning back or forward, turning inwardly or out...

φ

He does not care that he can't bring to mind so much of what has brought his mind to being capable of bringing anything to mind, but for the fact that such a history revealed is still a passage in the diligent surrender of the I he's come to think of as his seity, his own — his surrender to surrender, to surrendering again; that the set of all that's missing from his tally of distinctions is greater than the aggregate of what has been forgotten, what was formerly in thrall but now is freed, dispelled from view...

φ

What he's interested in now, despite his many odd distractions to the contrary — the many new temptations to take back what was never really his...What draws his interest now is that the world he's since omitted—still acknowledging its stamina in raveling his glance—is near in its presentiment...its absorption of presentiments...near the world he's entered into such a rough-hewn cast. There seems some useful analogue between what he's since registered as the infinite deferment of all disparate registrations and the intrinsic limitation of the ego that recalls, and so he hopes that solely by suggestion...that by this sole suggestion he might discover something new about the latter, what he knows he knows concerns him for good reason—as a brand of comprehending his environs, his terrain—and how he's fought to live it, how it meets his...

φ

He remembers once again what he has never once forgotten, what he's merely kept *at distance* from the present cursive cull, that what he yearns for more than anything is to understand how he's been thrust into such fraught inversion, how he might soon redress it, and avoid descending further should the chance arise. Yes, he has a purpose, he has always had a purpose, he wonders what it would be like to move on...to move *against* the reverie of setting goals—of gaining ground or anabasis—but not sufficiently to set it as a goal. He's somehow always managed—a curiosity, he thinks...He finds it curious he's managed to make headway in the service of some...some *manifest* objective; that he's made himself move forward while remaining in this purchase, while seeming to turn every fitful twitch towards something else...

φ

An unwitting distinction, one he's not precisely making; a distinction he's not sure if he's inclined to make at all.

He does not want to make it—so to take this reckless tangent—but he's come to understand it as a curve set in the highway, a turn he can't avoid if he's to keep along his present course...

φ

He does not want to take the time to explicate the difference he's discovered...he's *made evident* to no one while following this line. True enough, he thinks, were he the sort of dolt that most are—that he conjectures most are—he would simply find a method to distract himself from following...a way, that is, of shifting his attention to more pleasant—if less pleasing—approbations in the roadside ditch. If he were only just like they are, like the others...

φ

As though he has a motive to suppose himself thus knowing, to think he comprehends what makes the common fool...the common *conformation* of the common fool common enough to generalize to every last exemplar of the species who possesses it most fully—to make of every predicate of character the practicum and portent of a sovereign goad. He does *not*, he recognizes, have experience of persons *in general*...who in general one might call the common variance of common folk, such that he could make good on the promise of eluding all obeisance to ease and least resistance, to the following of virtues more imperative than what presents as preference, as preferment—imagined as the rarefied refractions of some avant-garde refinement or a facile acquiescence to the latest trend...

φ

He thinks if he were only just like most are he would never have found any way to skip this daft divergence—the gratuitous assertion of that singular whose sanction he imagines he would win if he could carry on. He thinks that if he manages to *not* further examine why he thinks himself so different from those he thinks would take a different line he will succeed in justifying why he thinks himself so different, that refusing to exemplify...to *express* his certain difference from those archetypes he differs from, *against* his lack of evidence—the absence of all argument in favor of his petition or its contrary, that is—exemplifies the ways... the many ways he differs from...

φ

He differs from all others, he surmises for no purpose... for no purposes but his own...He thinks that he can demonstrate his difference from all others by the fact that he surmises for no purposes but his own, but this is only one of many discrepating features, and not the one most curious...most *apposite* the portion he descries himself in now. *His* difference lies in his unwillingness to loiter on his difference—a difference here disclosed...*brought up* by his refusal to refuse to reveal differences he finds uncomfortable...uncomfortable *to show*—perceiving that such dalliance would prove the very obverse; that he was more concerned with comfort than with some ostensive terminus he tenders as the paradigm of true resolve...

φ

He's not that sort of punter, carried forward in the brume, who'd rather take on water like a ship's hull in a torrent than be forced to find his shelter on some common shoal. If he were like the others, like the others...He's happy to

entailments—*consumed* with the caprices of the world one's forced to view—is no more able to make something else receivable—to make anything of anything but that, but that alone. At least when what one fashions...one *discovers* at the center that's prevailed through such dissemblance is revealed as inexhaustible...*reveals*, that is, the inexhaustibility of everything that's ever been distinguished from the given, from the endlessly proliferating farrow...

φ

What perplexes him—what *excites* him towards this one of the assorted ends he's thus been forced to finish—is the *fact* of multiplicity, that what contrives the content of one's purview is brought to clear effect upon the faculties positioned to receive it, to *take it in*. Without the brackets drawn around one's fundamental vistas—one's appanage of predicates accepted, if perceived—there would be nothing possible to mention *or* to notice, no way to suffer through that superfluity of forms. Nothing would have form, he thinks, no unity of predicates...no class of discrete fragments made the axis of the whole would take place in the mind's eye or in the body's circuit, for drawing each its infinite of incremental movements towards a depthless void...

φ

Choice requires notice, purports choosing between choices, which is to say that choosing means not only the rejection of what one *hasn't* chosen but the coincident omission of a world...of those *aspects* of a world that never came to seem specific, those infinite surrenderings of infinite distinctions to the absence of a center, to the absence...

φ

He won't hazard thinking through it—thinking *as* it and so through it—one more time. He notices, that is, that continuing his chronicle of what's gone by the wayside—what's found a way of foundering in every wayside gulch—was what first introduced him to this posture—the tear to eye the sleeves to face the head so close to ground…He *remembers* that remembering what he's made sure of not forgetting for so long he can't remember having come to such resolve is what has led him to this lumbering attempt at postulation, the unremitting standards of his breathless vow. This time he'll remember to forget what he was doing, to turn back from his turning, from his turn back towards…

φ

What brought him to this moment was the *concept* of forgetting, the constitutive assumption of a world that's been forgotten without ever having known it—without ever proving knowable *to him*, after it's gone. What is, he thinks—what he believes still possible to realize, so to claim a knowledge *of*—ceases to be possible as knowledge *had already* once that moment…once *any* time has passed without its happening within his view, a difference made most manifest by this assumed distinction of what's not recalled *at present* from what's *never* been held fast in that mimetic swell. What one has failed to heed—what has been *banished* from attention—is not figured against purpose or redacted by delay, and so is not a factor in conceiving of the world through which one's sovereignty is realized; by dint of which one's stasis is directed, so *inclined*…

φ

What he means…what he *thinks* he means is this. He's not sure what it means that he means what he means; what *more* his meaning means, that is, or what other than he means he means by what he means to mean at any point thought present or thought through, but he believes that this...*this* this that is to follow, so to argue nothing more... he thinks this a beginning, and he's never once refused the opportunity for a fresh start...

φ

There are things he doesn't know, a claim he thinks he's well established, and even though he doesn't know precisely what they are, he knows that *some* of what he knows surprised him on discovery, thus recalling—now he knows them—that he didn't know them sometime, that sometime in the scope of his awareness he didn't have a knowledge of what he knows he knows right now...

φ

There are things that he knows now he knows he's lately come to realize, and by extension he endeavors there are novelties unheralded within him and without him, that every passing moment betrays new information that he *could* soon claim a knowledge of, no matter if he wants to or he does. All to deviate around that empty derogation so familiar to anyone who's ever had a proper thought, that what one doesn't know can have no substance—can't be *proven*—for the absence of the supplicant's ability to give it name...to *name* it, thereby call it out. There are some things that one might think one knows wholly...knows *completely*, but that sense of easy certitude—of languor in achievement—is always false, is at best a way of saying... of *asserting* one knows all one needs to know about such standing fore...such *propping up*...

φ

It is his contention—the very *groundwork* of his doctrine—
if he can be believed to believe anything at all...It is his
conclusion on the basis of the world that meets the margins of his liminal opprobrium that no one knows completely even *that* one knows, let alone the habitat in which
one's knowing happens, which must remain, he thinks
he's shown, forever undisclosed...

φ

And again. The class of things he knows he knows includes
the limits of his know-how...*implies*, that is, the things he
doesn't know and never has. But in addition to his fealty
to this physics of inclusion he realizes...he *remembers* here
and there, or when the circumstance allows, that there are
things he once knew well but has since lost in his reflections, that somehow such a litany of certitudes accepted
must account for what's gone missing just as well as what
was never there...

φ

Thus *two* ideals of absence prove confounding to his system—that which has been lost...which was at one time his
possession, and that which was omitted from awareness to
begin with, the first needing an entrance into signal collocution, the second acting as the fluxing limits of that turgid cull.
What he wants to now account for—what compels his sense
of provenance in counting anything at all—is what he's lost
to what's as yet an unwitting elision, that sense of where he
is, and who—to satisfy his means—he has become...

φ

He needs to understand those profuse reservoirs of know-how he once knew but has forgotten—has exempted from recall until this tractate bore them out—and those that he may still know still not knowing that he knows them—that *he's realized* that he knows them—so remain outside his dithering accounting of accounts...

φ

He knows that there are things he doesn't know by knowing that the things he knows he doesn't know completely; the sense at once included in his acts of knowing and his knowing acts that there is always something more, an infinite of unaccounted singulars racked up to supernumerary verve, so the similarly impertinent conclusion that such overage is the only way he can explain...can *require* what seems otherwise an indomitable megrim; that there are things he doesn't know he knows that he *will* know, things that he knows now that he has either never known or never known he's known before...

φ

There is an idle weight that's pressing down upon his shoulders, a weight that seems to increase with each moment he endures. He has his theories...he's able to *theorize* some general whim of natural order, in which this sort of shift in weight and subsequently register is needed to account for *any* designation of an unseen world. He's able to suggest the means to know that this would happen, a means he's never once employed, and so the claim is new, the claim is...

φ

How would things be different if he'd done as he *might*

have? He did not quite decide, that is, to take this stance or pose, but being nonetheless immured in such fell mire, he's fearful that its leaving…its leaving off *too soon* could bring about his *future* failure to keep stridently afloat within the cataract of references, the spate of opportunities that buoys his dank girth…

φ

Undeterred by all this…this *hesitation*, concocted as demurral, he wants to give it a go, see where explanation takes him, with hopes of fecund access to some otherwise *unthinkable* resolve. Here he is…he *shows himself*, he's never been here often; he *has not been*, it seems to him, so far as he recalls. Here he is inverted, head just inches from his mooring, when usually he keeps it up a distance of some yards. Some feet, at least, and then some, not knowing just how tall he is, what stature he's unwittingly assumed…

φ

Not only is there cause to understand such finite measure — the length from fallen arch to indurated fontanelle — knowable by practices untried or undiscovered, but it's an undisputed *fact* that he has segment and diameter, that every one or thing contrived extant extends *by definition*, insofar as every every is a one…

φ

There is no doubt that all such finite range is measurable, without consideration of having measured it as such. Yes, there is a codicil of things he doesn't know as long as there are things extensive, things whose gauge has never met his fancy, or his puerile wont…

104

φ

And more than that, there is this unrelenting…this *escalating* brooking of his burden as it augments, a weight which no appraisal of dimension would do anything to clarify at all. There is so much to this rancor, so much more than what such weights and scales can mete out as description… can ever serve to render as his own *avoirdupois*. It's not that he would like to take the measure of his straining, to juxtapose the burden of his pate *before* this stand with what it's come to mean now that he's held it…now he's in it…what it's *attained* since he first fully made it his abode; that further he would relish any effort on the part of his admirers to reveal the constituent virtues—the *varying densities*—of his head and all its suppurating parts. He would *not* do so, that is to say, although he knows that it would please him; it would pleasure him immensely, but to what end he's not sure. He does not think the problem is…

φ

The problem is he does not think the problem he's affecting— the problem that he's having to abide, to travel *through*—is in the substance of his thoughts or in the stuff that fills his noggin, in the bulk or the persuasion of what's set inside his skull, but…

φ

There is a weight upon his shoulders that before hitting this pose he hadn't noticed—hadn't *realized*—so far as he presumes himself to know. As far as he remembers, there has never been…he's never felt the weight that floats above his neck press down in just this manner…with the force he feels is pulling him—and all his vital substance—towards the distant...the nearing but still distant ground...

φ

He means, he thinks, to explicate...he *explains* his need to explicate the seeming contradiction by suggesting that there seems a contradiction, by *noticing* the evidence that mounts on the behalf of his reduction of what first appeared the simple to its various and severalizing parts. He's aware that every measurable distance is not only some small extract of a nonetheless *im*measurable field, but from the wary pre-science of the member whose concretion precedes substance the odd foretop stuck inside it frames an inner in its own right, a middle whose surrender to the partage of sensation is as certain as the whole it acts within...it acts upon...

φ

His head, he tries concluding, is some distance from the molder, growing closer with the sense of weight that seems to pull it down. That's what the weight amounts to, he accepts as though a given—the effort that's required to maintain what he conceives of as his hard-won ground. And more important than such effort is the certainty he's failing, that he's failing in his efforts to keep upright in reverse...to keep his head inverted and aloft against the increase of the obverse force. All this he's only realized by the decrease of his level...by the level of his view between the gates wrought by his knees; not by nearness to the ground so much as where his knees are balanced—the comparison of eye level to knee level, that is...

φ

And now that he thinks *of* it—now he notices he's thought

it—he can give a voice to what he'd long assumed but didn't *realize*; can describe a view between his legs he had no sense of sensing—at least no sense of sensing in its full-ness, in its whole. It was not in his purview, he had never thought to think it a precursor to some next recall...

φ

Yes, now that he needs it—now that it seems to him *signifi-cant*—what he'd previously thought the passing into index of his posture and the bracket that his posturing inveighs he will declaim his one...his *only* measure of the drift of his comportment towards another fleeting precinct, a plunge into the sludge that clings to everything *but* him. It is this very plight that activates his recollection, that requires his acceptance of a memory that otherwise would not have been...that *he*, that is, would never have thought estimably real, thereby complete...

φ

If he hadn't ascertained the sense of slipping forward... or is it back, he wonders, it's impossible to say...if he had failed to spot that he'd accepted such a certitude with what decisively appears an acquiescence to a previously hid-den span, then so he would not ever have recalled it, and it would have been lost to any future sense thought now. *Some* of what's remembered—of what one understands as one's realizable recall—is entered in that summary by its presumptive urgency, by making such an exigence a pos-tural relation to each newly surmised sputter of an ersatz world. There may be other methods—most assuredly there are—a premise he must reaffirm in order to avoid further attempts to think this one form of surveillance as the only... the one and only method to engender recollection, the only that he's ever thought apparent, or appraised...

φ

He realizes that realizing he's drifted towards the bottom of his bearing implies some prospective measure that he's never acted *on*. It's possible, he thinks, that what's beneath him appears larger from this attitude, so more fully shows its detail; that if he were to see the ground from this vantage alone it would relinquish the ulterior design of its moraines. And now he would pursue just such a prolix iteration—he would give it up *to* parlance and *for* evidence of sooth—if it were true, if it were only in his power; if he had only ever had occasion...had the *foresight* to look forward, thereby down below...

φ

And he could do it now, could risk this further furlough from fixed balance and displace the increased weight upon his neck, but not only might it leave him without any means to compensate his likely failing carriage, he doesn't think that it would prove of relevance just yet. He has no recollection of the size of the particulate detritus set beneath him, at least not at his entrance into this inverted stance. He may, that is, have viewed the stunted gloam of arid meadows as his head assumed its station—as it slowly touched the nadir of its fitful, spastic slump—but he can't figure where he was within that motion when he saw it, so he has no sense of distance from his steady state...

φ

On such premises alone he can dismiss from further interest the expanse of dormant pestilence set statically beneath

108

him…that he *believes* extends beneath him as a futile deviation from his course, in favor of a summary of those discrete
conditions he recollects as other than he thinks they are at
present, even as he knows that at *that* then he was ill-fitted…
was *insensate* to the problem; that he had paid no heed to
that commingling of traits…

φ

He knows that he is closer to his origin—to his *substance*—
but only for that burgeoning mimesis moored within him,
that act of bringing back what he had no idea was lost. He
knows that it seems strange his panorama should gain
posture…*take position* in accordance with his purview only
after he has lived it—accepting that he doesn't know he
knows it just as well…

φ

That he doesn't know he knows what he believes he has
established—that he's capable of *witnessing* that deference to his hidden grounds—unconceals a vault he can't
get over…*that surprises*, however brief the time he's spent
in thinking it his current pose. He's astonished by his for-
tunate lurch forward into purpose, that he's thinking what
one has to think to maunder aft and on. He has at his disposal what he needs for his disposal…his analysis…his
recovery of requisite conditions to array, while any action
purposed towards the prospect of disposing it eludes him…

φ

He knows that he is closer to the soil than he once was not
by noticing the burden of his foretop at its bulge, but by
some inner state he knows he knows now that he's after…

he knows now that he knows, that is, by all that seethes before him, every twitch of his inversion writ against the supple constant of his viscous bounds...

φ

He recalls, now that he thinks of it, his first view through that bracket, his first befuddled vision of the world turned upside down. He knew that it would happen as he felt himself pitch slantwise and catch balance on the rails of his bowed ligatures, in turn held fast in footprints slowly worried from the marl. He knows that he expected...that he had an *expectation*, allowing him the certainty that any knowing now or then could not have been the first...

φ

He knows it's not the *first* first by the same discrete entailment from which he first deduced something implicit but omitted from his image of this evanescent stasis—that having since expected...*remembering*, that is, that he expected the inversion of the world...of *his image* of the world upon his bending down to knee height, he knows he must have noticed such an order heretofore...

φ

Alas, it seems a principle of cognitive implicature, as though the advent of such phrasing could expiate the cark of being turned. He's sure he doesn't care what turn of phrase or sanguine gruel invigorates his ardor, as long as that's just what it does, without regret, neither regard. He thinks that when a principle inviolate by nature thus afflicts him—when it hits him crossing lengthwise in his sally lake to loam—he's required to betray it...to *reveal* it

110

to himself if to no other, to understand its subtleties, above the clamant precedence of other goals. Even *this* hapless redaction appears a dictum salvaged from the slag heap of divergencies, the midden of lost causes that he marshals for a home; even now, he now realizes, he must choose to make the point that he's now *pointing to*—and not continue on with what first brought him around to this…this…

φ

There are *two* rules here at issue, as he understands it, and first he thinks he must pursue the second—the *most recent*—if he hopes to understand his understanding as presentiment, a feat he thinks might bring him some small measure of relief. He's not *sure* it's true, and surely such a surety would be his most desired end, but he thinks that there's a chance, if just a chance—the only that he's come across in nearing this attempt. He has nothing to lose, an axiom of which he's still uncertain; he hopes there's nothing left to lose…that there's nothing there to lose, or that there's never really anything…

φ

He knows that what he has to lose by failing to pursue this sort of precept once it's offered…once it's given to the prospect of correlative regard…He understands that what he hazards losing by his failure to pursue any such principle divulged as he makes progress—he *makes way* within his conduit, while searching its next turn—is no less an achievement of his purpose than what he'd need to sacrifice by failing in such failure, by refusing to continue without duly changing course. He has nothing to lose by thinking through this piecemeal dogma as it offers up the principle of his pursuit *as* principle—as principle in principle, and so more roundly furnished as a *doxa*, or a petty trust...

φ

Having nothing left to lose—or simply having nothing—is a state well worth the zealous remonstration of pursuit, a state he thinks he hasn't suitably accomplished, or hasn't yet convincingly sought out. Acknowledging his previous...*just* previous assertion to the contrary—that he has nothing left to lose by taking on these frivolous diversions and retreats—he is again aware that his condition is unstable, that even with his unremitting stamina and fortitude he's running out of reason, out of time...

φ

What he *has* done, he remembers, is surmise the general mandate that gives stamina to every tick and twinge he can administer as agent—and not, that is, locate himself the victim *of*, the outlet to some *transcendental* end. What he's managed to bring forward—to *tease out* from his adventitious penchant for pursuit—is the succor of a principle he must assume as proven—as the optimum of acumen he knows he *ought* to sanction, accepting just as well that he can't know it's really true...

φ

He knows there's much at stake in his confused procrastinations, his need to turn away from his recovery of nesting berth, but he believes there's really only one way to continue—in consequence of his peculiar burdens and reproofs—and that is by adherence to the ideal teleology of purpose in the total, in the whole to which his present tense—for first and last—avers...

φ

Understanding his comportment as a species of endeavor—some means to means that can't be manufactured or contrived—he's come to the conclusion he must operate on principle, and only after doing so can he conceive of other worlds...of other worlds lived presently...as he conceives the world he lives in presently...

φ

What he's trying to say—what he's trying *to think* of saying, if not sound as an alarm—is that he comprehends his world as a divergence from its substance, from the project that the action of a subject stuck within it makes intrinsic to its being-as, thus any world considered as a being-as at all. He thinks that if he did not first accept a guiding principle as footing for his leap into the outside—the *beyond*—he would never have made progress in his pursuit of presence...his efforts to exceed the fungibility of his otherwise capricious whims. He must act as though the portent by which motive seems a possible subduction of the changeless real is realized; must act as if it's *possible* to act...

φ

One can only start out in accordance with one's purposes—and thereby come to substance as an actor in the scene—if one considers one's interior subsistence...one's inviolate *propinquity* impossible to contravene, thus one's *last* resolve. Such model of a subject needs the seity complicit in that vacuous comportment be assumed always at level, always filled to overflowing, to its utmost brim; that the person of each anima extend over a bracket always equal in its span to any other, whatever the position it must severally endure; that over every actor and each action in its habit hangs an *a priori* equipoise, a speculative rule; that the focal point of any claim to individuation is a subject that has nothing left, for never having anything...

φ

Of course he's always realized—he's never *let* the plaint escape him—that such certain equilibrium—such consecrated stasis—not only means that nothing's lost, that nothing's there for losing, but also that no profit can be meted out to substance, that being as an actor in the midst of such immurements means that no act can be justified by aiming towards a gain...

φ

He knows that knowing there's no loss established by position means that there can never be a gain to lose...to lose again...and so the inconvenience of his own craven coercion—of achieving *any* means to active purpose in the now—pursues him with a torpor in which he alone will flourish, a languor in which he alone will thrive. He believes that if he doesn't cede to every divagation he will lose an opportunity—a chance, perhaps his only—to resolve what's most abidingly his warrant in this bearing, in a world since born...

φ

He's attempting to suggest...he *is suggesting* a distinction— that within the world in which he acts no action but his thinking on the nature of such action can effectuate advancement, that nothing but *not* thinking about loss can effect losing, whatever stake that placid lapse appears to manumit...

φ

But perhaps that's not it either, he now thinks now that he thinks it; now that he's thinking *of* it it appears to him that acting in accordance with his general view that nothing's ever ventured by the enterprise of *thinking of* can't readily account for his position at the moment—the countless supplications that justify some postulate of contrary intent. Does he not experience the heartache of his billet so abruptly taken over, being occupied by so many vulgarians in turn? Does he not still long to know how this has happened to him? How he has been so roundly thrown into *this* disarray? And if he does...

φ

Even now he feels the pain of what he thinks he's losing... what he'll have *to do* to regain cloister on his perch, and as such he's assured once more of thinking his life matters, that his actions on behalf of his uncertainty are competent to vindicate each consubstantial jerk towards apposition; enough to make the thinking of his thoughts—insofar as they distract him from such purpose and pursuance—appear another detriment to bounding towards...

φ

If somehow there is something...there is *some way* to make progress, then he's sure that he must take it before the chance is lost. But all the same his vision of pursuit includes the principle by which his vision of pursuit has here been brought to bear upon his circumstance *in principle*—has been deduced to suit his present circumstance in full— and so with corresponding weight...with cognate *foresight* proves the need of such pursuit of principle...

φ

It is an odd fact of the cosmos…of *living in* the cosmos, as though he could avail himself of yet some other choice… an odd state of immersion that alleges…that *requires* separation in the substance of one's seity—of the ego in whose name one's action acts, one's taking takes…Strange one should distinguish between cogitative vigor and those exploits one effectuates by muscular restraint; between inceptive eidos and the foment of corporeal effect…

φ

Such conception only *happens* if each act of cogitation is distinguished both in fact and kind from that which holds the body in its midden of reflexes, as evidenced by nothing more than…nothing *so much as* the coincidence of disparate states within the selfsame subject, regardless of the content…what the last and best *accomplishment* of…

φ

All of which determined by the quickness of his facultative processes, processes he first discerns as reasoned by reflecting on the predilection by which he's disclosed, and so evinced. The character—the *attitude*—of what he gains or loses—all he chances losing by his absence of a native stance—is fitted to the speed with which he prosecutes his every act *ex cogito*, that in the passing suppliance to each untoward excursus he maintains a sort of balance in his posture and his view…

φ

The problem is the stretch of time between what he's decided to decide and his first move towards its attainment, its subreption by disposal in the cordon of an end; that he can't think his thoughts without expiry of *some* term, a quantum that's collated—that's established *as a limit*—by its making something happen, its being *consequential* to his prospects in the world. The commonweal he's choosing is not static while he bides it, thus what he's deciding is in part decided by the time it takes for him to make the choice to make the choice...

φ

The difficulty he observes in mapping out his choices—in describing those scant intervals in which he's forced to choose—has led to an expansion of that very same palaver, such that in the time it takes to...to *take stock* of his circumstances circumstances change, thereby cleaving present troubles from those dreams that once impelled him to take *this* affective course. If only he could think thoughts out of time, and in an instant...

φ

And how does he evaluate the passage as it passes? How is it he knows that any time has passed at all? Surely, the alacrity with which he's come to understand his tremulous predicament—the strained interiority of his suppliance to tilt and term—has nothing much to do with what he's suffered over that same pause...

φ

Isn't it conceivable that everything he's thought up to this point in his remonstrance—from the point of his first foundling blush to this point here and now—all happened in an instant, in the flash of an instant? And so he is reminded of what brought him to the question of the passage to begin with, his sense of something happening around him... beside him...of something having already and against his efforts *changed*...

φ

He gazes through the pillars that inscribe his stretch of vision, and remembers, he remembers, that there's something there that's missing, that he expected something else...Every expectation of resultant change or sameness— of deviance or maintenance, any way at all—is conditioned by the memory of that frame it presumes the likely circumstance it faces—is *conditional*, that is, on some remembrance of a setting, even if that memory...the *image* that that memory presents proves wholly wrong. Likewise does surprise adduce a reference to some fault in some dissembled recollection, some claim to static survey where the given world presents a succedaneum of corresponding frames, a conclusory exemption from...

φ

Expectancy, he understands, can't happen without knowing, without thinking that one knows what's come to pass, and *coming on*. One might not know what one knows as the sooth of some arrival, might think one apprehends some subtle schema that proves false in its arrears, and as such think again...and *tell oneself*, he tells himself, that what one knew was not a form of knowing, but of disregard...

φ

And even *this* distinction is not rightly thought irrelevant to what he'd like to think his ruling state, his future…He may be wrong, he thinks, although he doesn't like it; he doesn't like to think he may be wrong in what he likes to think, but realizes his thinking he's mistaken in pursuing such assertions has led…*will lead again* to just the same confutative conclusion; that thinking he's gone wrong in this odd remonstration is enough to make reflection on its form seem more than profitable…

φ

He wants to know how he can come to think that he knows something that he doesn't; how he can claim that something's true then find out that it's not. Perhaps his asking *how* does not direct the right procedure, the inquiry most likely to provision a result; what draws his interest more is the discernment of the difference between notions of *un*knowing—between thinking that he knows when he knows nothing of the sort and knowing he knows nothing to begin with, from the standing start…

φ

It's not so strange to think…to posit axioms misleading when contrasted with the scene as it *arises*, thus finding one's presumptive truths confounded by the real. And *when* he's come to understand his knowing was mistaken—when he's proved his proof *invalid*—he knows as well that thinking that he knew it—the *corollary* claim, that is, to knowing that he knew—was as mistaken as the claim to know itself…

φ

There are times when one betrays a certain visceral proficiency one didn't know was present or could ever be

119

erased, and this seems of a different order, a subset of assertions—those which by the escapade of *coming into* consciousness are proved right. One cannot fail to know that one knows something and then find that failure failed; having the mistake revealed requires a performative—which is to say a *synchronous*—acknowledgement of knowing that one knows and knowing that one's knowing that one knows was as mistaken as what one thought one knew that's since proved false...

φ

This, it seems to him—this nearly *paramount* presentiment—is precisely the condition in which he's held at present, insofar as such immediacy has shaped his whilom bow...But that's not right, he thinks to reconsider his position; if he is *unexpectedly* disposed in his deportment it's not because he thought it would be otherwise at all. He was surprised, that is to say, because he had forgotten that the passage of this interim—of what feels like his *whole* life—in this posture of inversion would result in some slight change in the formation of that standing...of that cull of norms itself...

φ

Of a sudden he realizes he's neglected...he's *failed to remember* what's deceptively self-evident when it's thus realized again...Now that he remembers it, he thinks there are occasions during which it's possible to know what one can't know one knows—to know without the *knowing* that one knows—but that every bit of evidence in support of such assertion requires thinking that one knows it to oneself...

φ

And so he takes his shrewdness for enough of an incentive; enough to countenance his coming back to truant cause… His analysis of cause bears out his growing insight—that he's *always* first expected this to happen as it happened, that throughout all his reflections on his means to such reflection he should find this new predicament progressing…

φ

So as he recalled what he'd assumed he had forgotten… all he should have known, that is, to keep himself upright, the neck began to bobble and the head drift towards the landscape, the very same that buoys up his footfalls as they pass. It's no surprise to him that he should feel his febrile promontory heavy with tumescence, a balance he thinks sure to fail should he fail to proceed. Should he *refuse* to think of something else before his finish; before he firstly finishes this endless reel, this tilting strife…

φ

More importantly, he thinks, he's not sure how he's taken measure of this subtle change in stature, how he's come to disassociate the pounding weight of atmospheres upon his hapless pate with such a slow and steady slumping, with a loss of stable posture…*How*, that is, he'd calculate the distance from his start point to this froward bent, or how he'd ever think to find his place within it hence…

φ

He understands that this is a return to where he started, to what remains the cusp of his assured digressive poise. He realized long ago he's hit this disposition elsewhere—that somewhere else he's hit upon this pose and so can claim it as his own—but such a realization neither satiates nor charms him, he's just not that sort of braggart, who is taken with accomplishments he's yet to find a meaning for…a meaning in…who's ever thought the act of taking stock of his accomplishments enough of an accomplishment to…

φ

He knows that he's been here before, he passed this post already in the course of this travail, and returning to it now brings him a momentary feeling of surrender, of tranquility; a sense of ease he knows is never warranted…may be unwarranted, he thinks, but he believes he can endure it by employing his degenerative zeal. That he is here at all…is here *again* at all is not unusual…

φ

It's not at all unusual for him to recapitulate such difficult mimesis—to judge himself again at such considerable loss—but such a state can't keep him from believing this a moment to reflect on his good fortune—his good fortune in returning to the gist of his bad fortune, his peremptory capitulation to this persistent strait. That said—or that *conceded*, in a step towards an acceptance of his lot—he has at last accomplished his refractory submission to the wile of sensibility; he's felt all that he needs to feel…

φ

And so he gazes out upon his suppliant horizon through the bucking frame presented by the brackets of his knees. He gazes out between his knees, betwixt that further margin of the frame that frames his lookout, that circumscribes his oculus with something like an inverse…an inverted…

φ

What interests him, that is to say—what first brought his attention to this measure of his failing poise—is that it is comparative, as every other variation captured or received; that it's not some wan observance of the *counterpoise* he's after—he's now longing *to enjoin*—but the intimated delta of this perilous immurement, the term—and thus the difference—that his newfound mien implies. What he's seeking is that sense of what he had no sense of sensing, a world before the movement that the inverse view exalts him to discover, to dissemble, *to revive…*

φ

He recalls that the horizon warped the poles to frame his purview just above the knee and just below the verge…He recalls a time not long ago…it can't have been so long ago, he simply hasn't been here all that long…He recollects a spectacle in which the plain that escalates behind him— and the thicket just behind the plain that rises to the sky— appeared to touch that glaucous spume above the knee but still within the bracket stretched out widest at its turning, and making in an instant a comparison that might take others eons to accomplish…completing *instantaneously* a comparison of that bygone persuasion—a perspective he remembers without ever having noticed having noticed it in its inceptive form—with those fractured conditions that confront his senses now…

φ

He might have thought the movement of the whirling earth beneath him the determinant and matrix of such corporal transgress; he might have failed to understand the nature of his venery, of what he thinks is something like the trailing of a scent; but somehow every spectacle that led him to this *anschauung*—the subtle instauration of the world beneath his feet—requires that the change be squared with what amounts to natural law, not merely with the ardor of his novel...his both novel and returnless task. It's feasible, he thinks, if for the first time just this instant...just this moment and this once...it's feasible to counteract such recourse to the purchase of a stable whole—a total spread—but such unhindered parry necessitates one keep oneself...one *lock oneself within* the regulation of the singular...

φ

He's well aware one can attain such resolute conclusion without going any further in pursuit of true resolve, but that doing so obliges the detachment of that self-assembled reason from the sense it reasons with, it *departs from*; he can *imagine* taking careful note and measure of the increase— the declension of the increase—horizontal to the line of his bowed ligatures and limbs, but a vista thus uncoupled from all further sense of movement would require that this furtherance—made previous *or* hence—suggest no apposi- tion to that subject whose proportion undergoes it, makes it object; that surrendering to happenstance gives nothing to the sense of having lived within the borders of some permeable husk...

φ

If not for that uneasy sense which felt so much like ballast... that feeling that his empty skull was somehow being filled; if not for the impression that his feet had staggered for- ward, explaining the imbalance of his swaying to and fro; if not for having felt the need to understand the auspices by which this new scenario could…has…both could *and* has entrusted him with what appears a whole—the hunger to elude the fateful ending of this series, of this *causal* mull—he would never have had impetus to overcome that nearness and draw something like…*near*, that is, to insight from the passing view…

φ

All this to say he's certain that it's not the sky between his legs that's falling—that's drawing earth up to it, as a margin to the void—but his own degeneration that results in that skewed landscape, a shift not inconsistent with the dizzying tumescence of his bulging fontanelle. Still, it would not matter that he's since adduced a difference in the ration of his hindsight if he hadn't also realized that a parallel to that beleaguered change in state and nature was the filling up of what had once seemed vacant with… with *what*, he is in this case ineluctably unsure. That he has means to make comparison, recalling his nativity to contrast with the strain he's ever pushing up against…what *fills* the filling vessel of his addled breviary *in the now*…

φ

He knows that what he knows he always only knows at present; that what he's pioneered by peering through his fencepost adjuncts…by *knowing* that he's peering through the fenceposts of his thighs, is that over the entire length and throttled aspect of his stalwart supplication—his unthinking acquiescence to a ground set in the sky—he's been doing only that, peering without knowing that he's peering…

φ

In order to achieve some more conclusive form of know-how—to know that he knows what he knows he knows in *consequence* of knowing what he knows, what now he knows he knows right now—right now he knows he must have known what he had no idea he was still capable of knowing…what he was *unaware* of taking in as something to be taken in—that view in turn evolved to suit the course of his decline…

φ

If one can rightly claim the imprimatur of the delta—of some change in state or nature, no matter what remains the same—one must have *some* sense of the limit of the substance as it changes; must *identify* the brackets that delineate the compass of motility, that is, and believe them *stable* moments, as enduring through the vacuous superlative of *having been remembered*…

φ

He is aware, he thinks again, of that peculiar obverse in the nature of transcendence—of duration through the pageant of this passage through the seal—as each such attribution of the changement to a substance is at once a near assertion of a previous stolidity, a moment's past duration, past in fact but not in mind. If one is ever capable…has ever been made capable…

φ

If one has ever noticed that one's noticing the change, one will notice one needs *two* such static moments to receive it, to *disclose* it; to reveal there is a difference in some nature that endures. There are two nodes that endure through each ostensive change in nature, every change in state or nature...

φ

Perhaps it's more than two, he thinks, unsure if such accounting makes a difference to his project, whatever it may come to in the end. Every predication of a change marks some consistency established as a knowable appurtenance of judgment—the first being that person of the ego that claims gnosis, that thinks itself as knowing through the transit, over time...

φ

And once one has established that the seity that's knowing...that there's seity that's knowing...Once there is a seity that knows itself as knowing, all knowledge of a change in state assumes there's a beginning that's enduring—thus of known simultaneity—compared with which the present is perpetually new. There must always endure within the predicating subject a consciousness whose cognizance identifies the change...

φ

Within the captive selfdom that seeks penchant in such movement—in the *vector* between postures of such visionary lean—there must be a sense of origin, of immotile advent; one must possess the notion of a nature that was stable, the nature that was given for the trope to be born out. And so within the prime subsists a binary of references, a suppliance of corollary, independent terms—the first that marks the thing as it's recalled in its persistence...as it *persists* within the nature that the change in state recalls, the second as it's given in the moment of the insight, the moment the comparison is patent, thereby made...

φ

In *this* case, he continues, it's the *third* that's most apparent—the final span with which that trussed motility concludes—and the prime, he here reminds himself, is that
which thus concludes it, in whose bracket the convulsion
of such forms has been delimited, so intrinsically revealed;
what's still missing...what's *gone absent* from his summary
concordance of a general view is the correlate of presence
by which presentation happens, that half of the binary that
passes for the middle term...

φ

It's not precisely how it works, but that's not such a problem; it's not the middle premise that leads proofs to their
conclusions, but serves as the first premise of the next
purported stumble into such conclusive ends. Transposed
upon that frame the ever disregarded second—the missing
half of what he's come to think of as the second—can't keep
place in the middle, and soon occupies the same intrepid
stature as its still opposing third—the conclusory *return* to
what emerges in the moment as the content of what's presently at hand. It's not that there is premise or conclusion
here on offer; the premise and conclusion are identical...
are *interchangeable*, that is, without asserting a distinction
in the nature of the inference, or the final turn...

φ

He knows that he continues to confound all common parlance, that all attempts to unconceal this way of thinking
thinking to another...to *any* gawking dullard would serve

to make things...to make *matters* more confusing, but this concern seems prideful—if it isn't wholly feckless—for the fact that he is not aware of anyone...of anyone now present; that he doesn't think his knowing...that his thinking of his knowing has been transformed into knowing—into knowing thinking or thinking knowing—set beside...*outside* himself; that any other has a place...has *ever* had a place endowed for seeking...for *revealing* such essentially excessive and inherent dross...

φ

Even if he thinks it's possible—and in truth he thinks it likely—that someone else might gratify his disconcerted gaze, he still can't comprehend it's happening...how it's ever attained happenstance *right now*, at just *this* juncture, and so he has decided that a clarity of purpose where his own discrete and cultivated process is concerned is what's required for his object, for the reaching of his object; that no other remonstration has necessity in principle or in the near view. If only it were otherwise, if only he had ever lived his life through the surveillance—the *acceptance*—of the otherwise...

φ

Knowing that he doesn't know if there are others otherwise allows him to decide things...to make *choices* that those others can't consider in the passing of such narrow spell. Others may have other selves, he thinks, but that's *their* problem; others may have others to whom they must explain the dreary vanguard of their musings and their shrill dissimulations, but absent such entreaty...such *awareness* of a singular awareness towards whom his deftless viscera of vocables can be understood *addressed* he sees no purpose in retooling his most courteous prosthetic, the litany of shibboleths that brings his thoughts…his thinking of his thoughts into this…

φ

And so he takes a moment to compose his new summation; he must sometimes *for himself* review what's come to rule his thoughts—that there appears a second that's gone missing from his register, despite finding no way to mark its absence as a loss. He has his first and third, he thinks, his first that thinks a third as an inclusion, as a balance in which both a third and second are submerged, but still he can't discern a proper second in its quantum, a second that can be described as granted, as…

φ

Ever not the present is the second of duration, always as some vestige of mimesis, of redaction or mimesis; a vestige that's preserved by the associative praxis of the prime. He is, as such, the primary by having thus lived through it—enduring the mutations that have only been adduced by his persistence in retreating through the bracket every primary compels. What's intrinsic to this empty indication of transcendence, this closing of the rupture that the delta circumscribes…what's *implicit* in the closing is the opening, or rather, the *closing off* of what begins the set he's just concluded as a member…as a member*ship*—an amity that's always firstly proffered as reviled…

φ

And even though he can't quite place the place of his suspension, of the posture he began his very first inversion *with*, he knows it must be there, that he must have seen it sometime and so brought it into consciousness, where it has been forsaken to unwitting profit since. It is, he thinks, this course that's brought him forward to sagacity; he's aware, that is to say, that his exacting disposition in pursuit of mental process is peculiar only for the fact of his return to reminiscence on the absence that he nonetheless believes his present state...

φ

Still there is a difference between such understanding of an outright sensibility—the *interior* existence of what must remain outside—and the remembrance of that same redacted incident as happening; the forthright recollection of an image of *that* time. He knows he must have lived through some perspective that's distinguished from the tableau of inversion he's experiencing now; he's revealed it, he's *deduced* it, but can't make out a way to bring it back into his present... his seemingly *substantive* view...

φ

This, too, is not an issue he thinks critical to manage, if it's ever been construed as such a pertinent surveil. He feels certain—though that's all it is, a feeling only—that much else holds the same place in the captivating landscape as it perdures around him; he feels certain with a certainty more passionate than clear that just as every act of thinking must assign duration or impermanence to what it *thinks upon*, so must every next reflection manifest this dialectic—this trinity of ends to mark the passage once its done...

φ

He must, he thinks, have already experienced the constant—

the constant that the delta, at its *genesis*, entails—and the subsequent conclusion that he simply can't recall it...can't *remember* that alterity, even after his *deduction* of the same dissembled world that the discernment of the change seems to conceal...

φ

What he's sure he would conclude from all this dithering contrivance, if he could only stop it and so move on from its fray...is that this absence of some notice of proclivity— the void of such awareness that the vacancy *makes plain*— can be taken for the promise of a prospect, a solution; for evidence of just that same refusal to advance against...

φ

If one can't recollect the manifold minutiae that mark the situation, so far as those particulars have been rightly observed, then one can say that what was there before was unremarkable, and as such has no impact on the scrutiny it severally commands. Understanding that one's whereabouts are so distant from the stipulated ease of stable precept—of *sustaining* perch—is enough to glean that what one thought or thinks was present previous to this was not *as* this...was not *as this is*; that if it were, the proof is clear, one would have failed to notice it as disparate—as *discrepant*—and so would never have discerned—thereby *described*—what one can't help describing by by the activity of discernment...

φ

He knows if he'd been subject to this bounding set of accidents—and he knows that it's a set, that there is more to any scene than he can notice at a glance—he would know it,

132

would recall it, if nothing more have noticed at the time of his surrender to...his *showing up* for purposes he still can't allege proximate; he knows by the construction of the space that he *lives in* that if he is to reach the ground, or even to approach it...that as he motions *towards* the ground he must go through the space that lingers wearily above it—that constitutes what he has always thought of...what he *thinks of* as above it—no matter *what* he recollects or how he feels its pull. If he is to hit ground—if he is ever to *come to it*—with anything but footfalls, then he must travel through the one...what he believes the *singular* extension that precedes it, that *inscribes* it; and as he continues to approach...as he *resists* such a confinement—the confinement of a balance in inverted pose, without advance—he again becomes aware of where he is, of what confronts him, in proportion to...in *accordance with* the distance he maintains from every...

φ

It is a wonder and amazement what this droll examination of such torpid circumstances *from the aspect of eternity* confects. What a joy it is, he tells himself, as the import of his triumph comes upon him, marks his witness; as his blushing and impenitent surrender to the blinding light of reason here distracts him, so allegedly proceeds to its next rest. What a pleasure to pursue that which so many take for granted, to stumble on the ever new complexity of purpose that a lesser understanding can't attest. It is, indeed, a premise proved by that same dispensation—the same torrent of reason sprung from fallow mind, from chance result—that he can think the movement from unconscious supplication to the opening awareness of the ego, the seity whose strain such strained awareness introduces by wandering through that same licentious lassitude he predicates to others in the distance, thereby taking up his locus in the cosmos, so his shifting view…

φ

That's right, he thinks with pride more than the preceding amusement, he knows his purpose was not ever static for a whit, and no matter how far he has strayed in thinking his thoughts relevant, his aim—his novel causatum…what he thinks is novel in his causatum—is still unchanging, still amounts to the *re*conquest of his newly sullied nest…

φ

Still he understands this sense of temporal locution as a form of teleology, his maunder over distant ground and near as an addendum to what still remains his still unmoving purchase, that although he still has much to do, he still knows he can't fail. His delays may yet be endless, but that's not what failure means—not what it means *to him*, if it's not precisely clear. If it's vaguely clear, perhaps…

φ

To fail to reach an end is to have given up its reaching, to disclose one's image of it as an honorary void; he may have other goals—he almost mouths what he is thinking—but that doesn't mean some order of redoubtable causation can be supplanted by another, something different and so new. There are more than enough orders to account for all his fractious whims and affable mutations, more than enough conjugants to reckon every subtlety he's ventured thus to venture to…

φ

At least he has this surety, if that's his only boon; the surety of finding sets and subsets in his purview, and even as he sights the flitting shadows of his yet inchoate terminus the radiance that casts them remains fulgent in its reticule, as such appears discernible, if not thereby discerned. A strange metaphor, it may be, and one that's sure enough as reminiscent of the sun...of the memory of the radiance that led him hencewise in the first place to return him to that futile plea...

φ

If only this *enough* were in itself enough to draw him, if only the catastrophe in which...*towards* which he finds he's driving were so easily refused a proper place within his portion, in the portioning of causes he might have another choice. But enough *is not* enough, he immediately relinquishes, enough to justify a choice in no way guarantees that one is able to go through with it—with the variance of making it, or choosing not to choose. There are always other aspects of one's aspects and desires that preclude such glib motility from pressing towards...

φ

And even *this* entelechy—the portent of his manifest decline—remains far less compelling...less *important* to him now and to his sense of purpose than the aching inflammation that is dilating his skull. Not his mind, mind you, not his thoughts, he thinks, but what fills the space between his imbrued ears and battens down his throbbing membranes, the load that keeps him stable against pulsing back and breach...

φ

There are, no doubt, those prone to the confusion of the substance that one carries as a millstone—that one drags as if in tow—with what engenders one's reception of the setting one encounters as an orbit of sensation, thus the omphalos of feeling that the sense organs endue, but he's never quite been one of them, and this new opportunity—this rut of interstices, of intrinsic interstices—seems to him the rarest of all involuted breaks—an unprecedented chance to trace the measureless distinction of what *is* as hapless sensor from the litany...the *cataract* of sense...

φ

He's certain he's uncertain that he's had no other chances, that he's missed every occasion to blanche in the receipt of such demurral—such *remonstrance*—but he's yet to seize upon just one such chance set in its moment, the notion hasn't *seemed* real, though neither has it...

φ

But that's not precisely it—not precisely *his* it, so to specify the plaint. He *thinks* it's it, that is, but he can't shake the premonition that his reasoning will somehow prove in excess, be *left out*. His *mode* of reasoning. He seems to just have claimed to just have thought up other chances, and thereby to have named them, as they *are* and as they've been; to have inherently *discerned* them, held them *subject* to the process, if that's really what it is, if it's ever really been conceived processual...the process of conceiving the processual...made a captive to the process of discernment, then recall...

φ

He has no recollection of those other circumstances, and so he wonders why he should assume that they've occurred—that they've lately come upon him, have played subtly upon him, in any stance or pose. The answer, he decides before he even asks the question, is not as easy as it first appeared—as though such vain dissent were not *itself* the first appearance, the advent of the advent; as though there were a *moment* when he could have seen it true and clear... clear and distinct—a turn of phrase that signifies a bearing, not a substance; a posture, not the fated affectation of a will. This may well be the very first he's thought that it's apparent—that he's found a way to feel it, as though it were a prod—but that hasn't kept him from the coup of having expectations, from hoping that it would not soon require the attention that it has done, that it does, or that it...

φ

One hopes that one does something—one does *everything*, perhaps—in order to make progress towards some pleasurable stint; some clarity of purpose that most fully and most frequently occurs upon the thinking...the *arrant* thinking of it—so to say as much to think...

φ

One wants to think what's true is also most clear and distinct, but it may not be so, he thinks, for realizing such clarity of vision hasn't hit his foresight yet. Not yet *now*. That this should still result in something like a novel concept—a *revision* of the idea of what's valid and what's not—has not escaped him, though that doesn't mean he'll reach it—that he'll take it for his own thought—and in fact he thinks he won't. In fact he will do nothing to conclude this proper vision, this vision of the proper, this...

φ

One wants to have done everything one does—that one *has done*—for those same explanations one imagines would surrender any other to the cause, if not the causatum—those that every aim proscribes to reach replete fruition—but it seems that there is something that stops everything from ending, no matter what the actor does to service such surrender to the closure, the *conclusion*...

φ

In *this* instance, he speculates, he'd hoped to come to terms with his insistence on the dearth of the substantive here in question—of the corollary predicates under observation hence—by revealing what he thinks the most convincing of all grounds for thinking such occurrence accurately fashioned—limned by thus concluding that it's never happened otherwise, that there has never been another means *to happen yet*. The problem, once again, is that he doesn't think it's realized, but rather an assertion on the brink of some default—of revealing what it's stolen from the *true* portent of certainty, something that it's never of its own accord possessed...

φ

On the one hand, he assumes he has not settled on this verdict because he is *convinced* of the singularity of the chance—of his chances of revealing what's at stake in the conjunction of the sensor with the action of his *feeling*, of his sense—on the other he still understands that thinking some one scene occurs more frequently than never, and only on this one occasion has been thus advanced—duly predicating rarity not to happenstance but seizure—requires for a proof the recollection of conditions as they happened—that are, as such, in evidence—and he simply does not have... cannot *describe* that recollection; he simply can't collect it from his posture or his lurching prance. So why has he accepted this conclusion as conclusion? Why does he believe the gamble *possible*—but lost? He has a guess...

φ

It is *this* wizened meeting place that he alone has occupied... that *to his knowledge* he alone has occupied, he thinks, where reason and sensation not only conform easily, but where some act of reasoning bestows its pulsing datum with alterity, with status; where the world he lives meets up with the conditions that make any world a possible...a possible...

φ

That some one world is possible doesn't mean it's happened—that it's risen to existence, whether divulged or covert; it's a judgment that requires neither case nor iteration, but he must still remind himself...here and there he recollects in what reside his limits...*of* what he might trip trippingly across if he's not clear, for having done so otherwise, in some erstwhile travail. That any world is possible is astounding enough; that any one world *in particular* should have slipped into this speculative pale...

φ

He lives a world that holds within the precincts of its purview—the magnitude of what it is, and so what it excludes—conditions thought as likelihoods that function as the boundaries of what *of all* is possible, and what confects the signposts for the limits of the merely real.

What's possible, he thinks, is *sometimes* real—sometimes *existent*—but such pretense is equivocal when measured against fact; the actual, that is—or what's contrived one's living *of* it—implies its own modality, but there's nothing in the nature of such *possible* existences that opens up the present to a future world. Everything may pass away into an endless absence—everything does, he tells himself, in every setting one can understand as having been—but the prospect of duration he's already brought to notice marks its margins as the limits of the sensor who endures it, the subject whose cohesion is implicit in the sense. That said, the transition from proclivity to gnosis can't be realized without pushing the receiver into some distinctly *tractable* awareness—as though there were another sort, but still...

φ

The necessary, he presumes, requires no such evidence—no verifiability, no possible reproof—but the possible...well, what he *wants* to say...what he thinks, he thinks, is this; it *may* be taken for a certainty that this time is the first time he's first had opportunity to demonstrate what he hopes first to demonstrate—that he has never before noticed such performance or its imminent display—but to any *reasoned* seer this must seem a precondition so unlikely that it nearly proves the *obverse* of its warrant, a likelihood for all intents and purposes intrinsic to the world that it apparently decrees. Well, not *all* intents, he thinks; all *purposes*, perhaps...

φ

How is it possible, given his willingness...his *imperative* to follow form to principle, without regard to sacrifice of influence or chance...How could he come *so far* in his upsurge to existence—so far towards his majority, towards his declination towards...How could he have reached the impecunious conspectus of his present situation without having considered more discretely—more discretely than *not at all*—this specific problem, even if he can't recall an instance of its...

φ

If he has never before done it—if it is indeed his maiden sail through these impassive seas—well, he thinks, so be it, let it turn out that he's wrong. Either way he will regret it, either way there's no result. It is the principle conjectured by his reconsideration of the question—his decision to *assume* he has achieved this plight before—that is of interest in this moment; he finds it interesting, he thinks, though for no rationale apparent to him now. He may never have occasion to think back to this occasion, if he can ever manage to arrange for such recall, but there is a chance, the slightest chance, and that's enough to think it's worth it, even if he didn't think so when...

φ

What's more, he's come to realize, he'd already reached this doctrine before having deduced it; somehow he was already assured that it was so, at the same time holding no such recollection of his motives, let alone a proper fealty to...He can't recall his ever having come to this position, and yet he had reflexively...had *immediately* turned to that foul reasoning within him, as though it were within him...

φ

Besmirched by such foul reasoning, he understands why one would take the path that it invariably proscribes, but absent an awareness of those timorous locutions, he doesn't know how he could come...could *hit upon* the same procedure that he has after its end. A guess, perhaps it might be, but this answer's not quite sound; or worse, he thinks, it can't explain why at the time...the *instant* of decision—barely an instant, as he sees it, when compared to what it's taken him to reach his current frame—he was not only choosing one of multiple directions, each with kindred importunity, so to exit from this pose, but he was certain...he *felt sure* that what he'd chosen was the right way—chosen not for comfort but *for cause*...

φ

Is it possible, he asks himself, that somewhere in his past he's faced a similar conundrum—similar to this *form* of conundrum, if he can't be more assured? Can he apply the same to this same suppliant entreaty, the same he is interminably querying upon? There is a difference; in this moment—this *example*—he can find within himself no real desire...no *entelechy* to push towards the unreasoned final term, so entirely immured within the throes of the predicament that by the time he's able to discern it as a problem he's already past the point of no return. And what would happen if he weren't? If he could somehow reach here without passing through such inference—as his only rightful means to beat a path, to hold his realm? The question is too ludicrous to answer...to *dignify* with anything like direct response. It is perhaps the case that having seized upon this penchant for the ruse of probability—a reckoning enacted *by dissent*—he sees no cause to look back at the cause of his impulsions, to give up the decision to make choices on the basis of what seems a *likely* world, and not, that is, a world confirmed by having lost...*by having past*...

142

φ

Likelihood can't be construed as evidence of actuality; there are many things—himself not least among them—that are conspicuously *preposterous* but are nonetheless extant. Of course, this is itself a claim that *seems* to be self-evident…that may well seem self-evident *to him*, if no one else, but only for his own capitulation to expediency, to what amounts to nothing more than purview, than perspective…

φ

He's accomplished his obeisance to otherness…to testament…his unwitting subsidence *into certainty* at last. He realizes he may appear a frail and fetid cretin, that there are not so many such as he upon this path, and furthermore he plays a rather unconvincing vagabond to those who stumble by him, no matter how degraded, both in number and in wits. He may not know they're there, he thinks, he can't begin to think it; but in this case *what* he thinks—and so by inference *can*—is itself what he's directed towards the imprecated meddler he hopes himself to be, no less to fake. He knows, that is, that if he's hailed by anyone at all he's likely to be understood as deviant, as singular; a lone instantiation in his form if not his stance…

φ

Of course, from *his* perspective, his appearance in the nature he's encumbered…he's unendingly encumbered *by* is not just a likelihood, but an exigent constraint, and as such all these predicates that make him so improbable are what construct the bracket through which his allegations of such flustered probability are cast. He is—within this posture—the most likely of all persons to have gazed through the parentheses of buckled knees, and though he would himself be quite surprised to see another...to find another *like* himself in such inverted pose, he thinks it no more likely that the same replete perspective—if it is in fact still semblable, still identical *to itself*—can ever think that self as the most probable...the most probably extant of all that is...was...is...

φ

If the world is *part* constructed...*made whole* by the presumption of the seer *held within it*, then how can one remove oneself and still think it persistent? If the ego is constitutive—if perspective is asserted *to prepare* its perseverance—then such ego can't be taken from the prison it abides. And if one must have consciousness—it follows from necessity—then the same particularity without which such a consciousness is outright inconceivable is just as much required by the world at large. Not only must the selfdom that endures through such perspective hold as steady as the focus of the vistas it receives, it must accompany a personage, a temperament that can't but feign compliance with the portent of its absence, with a likelihood conceived as absent seer...

φ

Alas, this path is still so far from his accustomed purposes—from what he thinks the stench of present purposes *revealed*—that his pursuit would mean the loss of every other terminus, all other supplications to a promised end. He would still like to proceed with what he has proceeded with, but he believes that progress—for he knows that it's progressive, that his turning back is liable to result in some delay—will eventually surrender his position to intransigence, and usher him to something like an unbounded collapse.

He does not want to lose a train of thought that seemed so fruitful, so ripe that he can taste the scurf of rot pressed to his tongue. It's not that he believes he wouldn't make his way to this horizon in some other feckless future, but that he thinks it will be easy to alight there, while these lesser points, for what they're worth, may well be lost for good. If all roads lead to Rome, he thinks, then why seek out the shortest path, the truest line...

φ

And so a second principle...is it the second? And what, he tries to recollect, could he have called the first? The query is inconsequent as he won't dare pursue it, not because he doesn't want to, but because he doesn't care. Contrary to popular belief...what he *imagines* is the character of popular belief, insofar as it's revealed, one may want something...want *to do* something that one doesn't really care about at all; the thwarting of which, that is to say, has no appreciable consequence, no meaning besides wanting...

φ

Another wretched principle—perhaps, at last, the last; that he mustn't only push on in the hunt of some surrender—of his unrelenting decadence in form and thus *in truth*—but must also dodge all secondary following of impulse that may lead to *other* principles; that could possibly necessitate the giving up of some end that may have no chance of coming round again. He will not abandon one stance for the taking of another; he may look away an instant, he may blaze a virgin path, but he will only follow if he's confident he's able to return to that originary gambit, to that purview trained to meet his...his facile but *unmoving* glance...

φ

Where was he when he first took this second as a purpose? What was he thinking of back then when he began to think of...to think of something else, he thinks, whatever that was...that *would have been*, now that he's relinquished its pursuit? That's it, that's it again, he's always known that he would find it, and by knowing he would find it he has found...

φ

He knew he would remember what it was, insofar as it remained to him important, which it did, if evidenced by nothing but his willingness—his willingness in defiance of all contrary pursuits—to turn back to it, an urge he only feels...he only *experiences* when it holds for him some relevance to immediate predicament, whatever it may be. It's important, that's enough; and *when* it is, he recollects, he's always recollected *what* it is, and who's revealed it; remembered how to mount it to the slope of his regard...

φ

The question, he recalls, is how he came upon the answer absent knowledge of the question, thus the means to free its speaker from the yoke of such ingenuous repute. What is a claim to exigence—what does it *amount* to—after it's been fixed in purpose, incrementally surpassed? What does it mean to want for what one already possesses? To shelter in an absence that's been pictured as complete? So does every query spoor the same formal conditions as the simple prosecution of a simple need; so is every question only rightly met with answers that sufficiently allay it—that constitute an adequate accession to its predicates—if

such discharge yields the state of ease that antedates awareness of deficiency...

φ

In this sense such sufficiency delineates all subsequent surrender to fulfillment, thus the sense of *in*sufficiency initiates
the asking of the question to begin with, so its answering
in substance and in turn. Conceiving of the problem—of
the absence that needs filling—is what brings the question
forward—what necessitates its asking—compelling the in-
quisitor to take another course...

φ

There may be no real chance that he will answer what he's
asking; it may be unlikely that he'll ever reach that end, but
distinguishing such perquisite from some mere curiosity is
that one can't...that *he* can't help but ask it in its moment,
at the time that it seems exigent *to him*, on present course.
He wishes it were otherwise—he may wish it were otherwise—but...

φ

So what precisely is it, this imposture—this *ecstasis*? What
primal indecision still arrays his world with silence, with
this restive collocution while still saying nothing else—the
resting restive promise that allows him to return to every
resting obligation, every equipoise exceeded, or reluctantly
repulsed? He assumes—he has *always* assumed—that every
other declaration of such rational appurtenance, such reflec-
tive supplication of the excess to the whole...that all who
seem possessed of some correlative discernment are nonetheless incapable of what he is best suited for...what is his

very nature, thus he proffers as endowment, not deficiency...
that if they were like he is they could not *not* reveal it, just as
he is forced to carry out this pageant of deformity...

φ

He is not ever able to do otherwise, to *make himself* do otherwise, just as they can't do what he declares a state of common cause. And how is it he knows they haven't similarly set out, where he himself finds no way to proceed
but that he does? Why not think they are as fully capable
of scansion—for that is how he sees it, as the scansion *of the
world*—but that they've found a reason...found a way to
use that reason—the same that he's possessed of, so remains
immured within—to continue on some other path, to plough
some other ground? It is simply not enough to generalize
those moments—strewn few and far between, he thinks to
add, and so he does—when he has come across such others
occupied in otherness, and noticing their idle affectations of
a forward stride declaims they're not like him. It *is* in fact
quite probable, he thinks it's fair to say, that if it's possible
to straddle this encumbrance...*his* encumbrance of reason
with a choice of means or modes, then that's precisely what
they're doing, what they've always done, and so...

φ

He not only assumes otherwise—an extravagance of *faith*—
but he's sure of his correctness; he's certain that he's right.
What he realizes he's realized for some yet unmeasured stint
is that when his fateful project seems a fealty to his asking
of the question—to the question *rightly put*—it's not because
some other...some scant portent of alterity he apprehends a
threat has never seemed likewise commanded, but that out
of all the ends one can credibly pursue the only one that

stands above...that *distinguishes* itself from any other any way at all is that whose means are what *his* are...are *as* his means, a ruin—an *opportunity*—alone bestowed by chance. The proof of this, he realizes he realizes he realizes...

φ

If somehow he can make the claim convincingly—the claim that he's convinced himself already is the truth—then he must bring to consciousness—to the sense of his conviction as it's evidenced in sense—that necessity *by nature*, by being proved consistent *with itself*. He must believe it's not only desire that has brought about...that brings him *to* his purpose, but that he has some cause to think he's never had a choice...

φ

The problem, he is well aware, has somehow lead him back to where he started...where he started the decline to where he started...The problem that *he's facing*—that's *made light* of his inversion—is of the same abhorrent order as that with which...that problem with which his pursuit of *this* one first began. And in defiance of the prospect...the *improbability* of such occurrence having happened in fulfillment of some...of *any* estimable plan, he's sure that this has had nothing to do with what its object is; he's sure, that is, he did not know that such accord of means to ends would be his end, would be his goal...

φ

His standing mark, his ready pose, but only after coming to it, as an actor who's position on the stage has been *laid out* by common purpose, but not knowing its location must have faith upon his entrance that the target will be clear when he needs discern it most. He must find what he's looking for—must discern his portion—but in this case he has done so by avoidance of all system...of all systematic *program*, endowed with equal credence that only by this method will his blocking...his next *aim* be unconcealed, as though by rote...

φ

He has stumbled on his mark, he thinks, within present paresis; has fallen on the gist of his odd stumbling about by simply noting, as he has...by *having noticed* that the gest he thought would leave him in another desperate scramble to look back at his arrival has brought him to his purpose with an urgency he's never before felt. Not thought, he soon corrects himself, he thinks he's sure he didn't think it, notwithstanding thinking so a moment...but a thought's beam in the past. He did not really think of it, of what would soon encompass his demeanor of abandon...his feeling of abandonment again, if not at first...He did not *only* think it, he expected it with what he thinks the panic of subordinate surrender, thus assent; he's come upon his purpose without effort, without *appetite*; he's met his sloughing groundwork, and it pleases him to no end...

φ

He knows that he can't tolerate such apodeictic harbinger—his joy subsides the moment that he hits it...that it hits him; it is as such *accomplished* at the instant it's received. The end of joy, he theorizes, is always the beginning...the beginning of submission to some next resolve. Now he's seen his place, he thinks—and mastered the new balance that such installation spurs—there's nothing left to do but hear it out, but see it through…there's nothing he can do but now continue on with it, which is just what he is doing — what he has, in essence, done. By thinking that he must return — by learning of his absence from the urgency to which he pays his paltry alms — he's learned another method, he has found another mode, a method to find method without mode…

φ

How else could he have known that he must do what he's doing, when doing so requires he repudiate the rest of all that *could* be thus pursued? It is just the sort of trouble that he's on about…that he's been going on about, attempting to release it from this petty swoon; there are so many necessities — so many *certainties*, that is — that he's accepted while acknowledging he can't recall the time or means by which they were revealed. They have not been revealed, he thinks, perhaps that is the answer — they've been *discovered* by the accidental turning of his glare upon the problem, as a miner who hits pay dirt despite having no reason to beseech the ground *just there*…

φ

But that's not quite it either, not so near to his return; it's only pressed him backwards to another fraught torpidity, another groundless claim to having reached his proper form. Discovery, he thinks, is but a type of valuation, whether that lost dupe to whom such truth is granted has approached the point with sifting screen and shovel's hasp or subtlety of eye. There is always such a moment…one such moment of discovery…and even if it's missing from some catalogue of readily accessible impressions it's still certain that it's happened…

φ

He imagines there are many varied instances of knowing whose portentous subjectivity—whose critical *singularity*— is hardly given *any* shrift, let alone the short, and even as he knows he doesn't know just how he knows them—or even *that* he knows them, when they clamber to the front—he hopes his fetid cargo of a corpus let's them pass by without notice, and moves on...

φ

Alas, a slipping step, a choking belch, and he is soon enough abandoned—a suppliance that's always first contrived as *once again*; abandoned to that same peculiar incident whose exigence first brought him to the asking of *this* question—the progress of his gradual...his gradual but still *limitless* decline. He slips a bit from what has been... what's proved his stable balance—balance for perhaps a far sight longer than he ever could *expect*—and so the slight move forward reminds him of that erstwhile expectation...

φ

A strange species of dyspepsia that yields such recrudescence, his momentary glimpse into the dangers of his likely end. He finds it odd, that is to say, that so many fractious layers of what bulks the very center of his still composite corpus, what seems to him the *substance* of the heritor of rights...that so many ardent and insuperable tangents are held central to the muddled constitution of the person who is speaking...who is thinking...

φ

He finds himself concurrently accosted by some multiple indignities that nonetheless hold no clear stake in precedence or cause. It's not that he can't think of any other form of ordinance…No, that's *exactly* what it is, he thinks, that if one can't describe two drives as causally related…as having been emergent to each its present moment of instantiated forms, then everything between them is proximity — is *distance* — in deference to the limits of the field thereby defined. He does not know if first he stumbled forward for no cause or if his eructation served to foreground that regression in adherence to his formerly abiding stand, a balance that appeared to be sustainable *until* then, that need make no adjustment to…to…

φ

Perhaps avoid the next lurch and the next, arranged in series. It's possible, that is to say, that his brief trip from impact into posture could have easily resulted in displacement of the dropsy that his desperate gulp relieved. And was such discomposure escalating as he lived it? Was there any reason…any *way* to have suspected that this voluble release would someday come? He's certain that it's not the first he's found justification for expression of such vendible imposture — that what he understands to be a product of digestion has come upon his variously cinctured portals and dissembled holes before — but as in every other act of mere instantiation — of discernment as familiar, as *repeated*, by design — it can be attributed…*deduced* as having happened prior to the jolt that brought his pith to such recall. He is comforted, he thinks, in the acceptance of this steadfast — if still unresolved — consistency…

φ

Which does nothing to explain the fact—the easy and ubiquitous lading—of such limits on the variable subject thus compelled to appear whole. He accepts that there is something in the nature of his naturing inseparable from what he is and what he has become, but he is just as troubled by a similar…an *indistinguishable* experience of understanding *after* the awakening…*his* awakening into this new guise…

φ

He finds it difficult to realize that such seeming realizations extend so far beyond what he believes his distant origins into a contiguity that never once…that cannot be related to a time before the verge that cleaves his present anamnesis from…to…both from and to his incult juvenescence—if he has really lived that sort of latency at all…

φ

Yes, he thinks in words that are not ever given, that invigorate his tongue without a thought to beat or pause, a certainty he otherwise reserves for *present* countenance, for what he thinks has only been quite recently received. Yes, he knows, this seems the very focus of the matter…of what matters to the form of this most formless tangent now— that somehow things he knows should be remaindered in abstraction; that even his expressions of mimetic cues in turn should only take form in occurrence…in perceptible embodiment, foundered on those norms he can't remember, but assumes…

φ

Who, in the performance of the most impulsive sentiment—or even the most genteel, he's not sure which seems more true—can recollect the learning of those standards in the first place? Who can give a voice to what's been granted such attention long before the hold of voice can be remembered, thus construed? Before there was a sense of the before of what comes after, of the after that has always come before what straggles after...

φ

But no, he tries to tell himself, it's all too much to venture—too much to try to tell oneself, too much to try to solve; he can't employ this posture of inversion to depict his inner semblance both as minimum and center, to explain what makes his every act of thinking possible—of thinking *thinking* possible—not only to express, but to receive. He cannot do it all, he thinks, and in his conformation to this ageless norm he knows he's not alone...

φ

One cannot do it all, he thinks with knowing resignation—thinking of so many paths, so many ways to go; he imagines there are others who confront the same awareness—a sense of what's still left to do, of what there is *to finish*, whatever marks the nature of that doing, or that being done...

φ

He imagines there are others who suppose their chosen projects—the cordon of imperatives that fixes them to goal—too extensive to be possibly completed in the time that's been allotted...in the *lifetime* that's been granted every personage in full. He knows he's heard the claim before, and as far as he can tell there is little that can set one's sights...can sight one's set *upon* that doesn't go too far to measure, far beyond what he thinks possible to think, much less to do...

φ

That such puerile expectations are configured as desires—that what one asks oneself to finish is nothing but submission to the path one *wants* to follow—can't stop the dauntless philosophe who thinks himself diviner from discriminating what one wants to want from what one wants—and what one wants, he thinks again, from what one can't *help* doing, which is always what one does, if nothing else, if nothing...

φ

One might as well have failed to fulfill any expectation held in deference to such temperamental longings and requests, whether such entreaty takes the structure of a vague vaticination or the pretense of an ought. The mere *notion* of imperative feigns an apt desiderata, even if its content is distinguished—is kept *separate*—from the prospect...the prospective *realization* of any *particular* want. One may try to do one's duty—to realize what one's duty makes compulsory, so does—and still not *want* to do it, have no way to act upon it, to transform it into static cause...

φ

He does not think that wanting more than one can have implies that what one wants to do is other than...*amounts* to more than wanting to do everything one wants to do and knowing it's not possible, knowing that one simply can't do everything one wants to do *right now*. It may turn out that some needs can't be synchronously sought for hav-

ing contrary requirements, that one must make a choice...
must *choose* between one craving and another, leaving
such excluded other absent sensate referent, so an empty
set. It doesn't matter if one should regard the incapacity
as ought or disappointment—as a thwarted expectation or
a target missed; conceiving of a realm that's always wanting...that's *left wanting*, notwithstanding what one wants,
can't help but hold the form and strength of obligation
proper, and signifies that wanting what one can't have is
already a projection of one's duty to complete the world...

φ

But he'd rather not get into that...*accede* to all that tumult,
it simply doesn't suit him to convey such a subordinate...
such a *secondary* determinant as prime. Yes, it doesn't suit
him, as if *that* were an expedient he'd use in making his
decision to turn leeward or let out the sail. His objection is
that every last...first or last to follow principle, the principle of following one's disparate inclinations into what one
thinks will make a more *companionable* vale...that every
valid argument can be read as obligation, or can't be de-
claimed otherwise; constitutes an ethic—a conception of
one's *duty*—whether such obeisance survives for but an
instant or endures over the whole length of one's choosing
life, one's life to choose...

φ

All of which reminds him once again of how he got here—
the interruption he was in the middle of when he was first
diverted...when he first *interrupted* his divergence with
this numbing dross. It's true of all our lives, he thinks, as if
he were a member of a set whose only...whose one *discriminating* predicate is the excise of desires like caprices, like

vexations; the straining of a temper without inner sense, a body without...

φ

There was a time before he came to knowing subjectivity — to realize his capacity for conscious *act* — when he lived as entelechy, as nothing more than sundering *by force*...He's reminded, once again, that he was thinking of that portion of his life that he can't think of, attempting to *fill in* those gaps that constitute the first blush of persistency, one's acting towards...

φ

What is interesting to him, he now recalls as if he's come to it, as if he's given himself over to receipt...What's interesting, he thinks, is that immured within this moment — in his always fully conscious state of poise and counterpoise — he carries out precautions he has no notion he's realized, of the proving out by efficacious knell. And even more disturbing, if the promise of such visceral distraction isn't clear...Even more *revealing* is he's *still* reaching conclusions without realizing he's reached them; still learning what he has no *conscious* basis to believe...

φ

He *knows*, that is, he's learned things since his primal incarnation as a learning thing...as a thing that knows he's learning things, and that some part of what he's learned he can't bring into mind; that some of what he knows he doesn't know he knows at present — nor that he has learned it — until he has the need to profit from his learning *of* it; until he finds it's being used...

φ

He finds he's using know-how—that he *knows* things, he believes—he could only ever learn from having evidence before him...*within* him, as a hidden scene. He knows that he knows some things that he doesn't know he knows by noticing the traffic of astonishments and hopeful jolts, that as he recalls thinking...*deducing* that each relevant and taciturn expectancy contrives inner *expression* of what reason such a one has to assume...

φ

But that sense, he reminds himself—that grasp of pain and comfort, however it's been ported to sufficiency, thus owned—is not consistent either; even if he'd chosen to pursue his many pleasures to their impulsive ends he's sure... he's *confident* for reasons that remain, as such, a lapse, a kind of void...he's certain with a confidence both born of expectation and necessity—of the *nature* of the thing, as it assumes its form—that his pleasures are themselves forever fleeting, at best a fleet capitulation to what he thinks the limits of a changeless world. Choosing what he wants— what to denominate as craving—is not proved a possibility in this redacted pose, and when it is accomplished without meaningful demurral he has every expectation of his lasting inability to satisfy the need...

φ

And so he ambles forward from this momentary craving, returned to what's occasioned by the absence of it's gain— returned, that is, to something that could just as well have bodied forth from any situation, something not impelled by indecision but *decidedly* an offering to chance design.

He would like to locate something—something *ontic*—to hold onto, which is just how it occurs to him...how it feels to him to think on worlds that might have been and *still could be* while making sense of every next attempt to keep his standing in the world he's in right now. Who, given his druthers, would not want to do something...*anything* other than *he's* doing? Who could have...could *ever* have conceived of this position as a form of right desire, as a target one would aim towards without some coercive strain? Who, given his druthers...

φ

And so he knows with certainty, no matter what else comes, there is no easy pleasure in his posture, in his carriage; that conceiving of his circumstance as an end in itself... an end that is not understood as *on its way* to something, but as a bastion in the middle, an axis that has never been conceived as anything but...Anything but something that can be described as anything or nothing, as either some or none, without distinction...

φ

What is evident, he understands, is that—having no object—he can't pinpoint what the nature of his object is... his *prospects are*, not when put against the cull of *possible* persuasions, persuasions that can be at once confected as results. He realizes that he still has *some* purpose, some *objective*—that he's only at this impasse for having lost his place—but such a realization has little to do with centering his will...his *inclination* on another novel aim—any aim conceived of in his present...in any somehow present state at present, or at all...

φ

He knows he doesn't know how such a bullock of a terminus is relevant to what he's doing while he stands his ground, and now that he's returned to just the thought of it...the thought of it...now that he's attempted to return to just the thought of it, he realizes he realizes he can't. True, he's found himself in some ambiguous relation to what first led him to this secret trove, this latent graft, but what that state amounts to—what it *is*, if that's his point—is just as utterly elusive to him now as what's behind him; is behind him, so beyond his grasp...

φ

Is it not conceivable that those who *had* betrayed him, those strangers who had thoughtlessly displaced him from his thoughtless...his *ungranted* appanage have since departed for some more propitious spectacle of status, what's sure to be some far more pleasant ground? Is it not a possibility, he joyfully avers, as full of hope as he can hope to be...Isn't there a chance, he thinks, that everything he's thinking— and as such that he's doing—should prove completely useless, perhaps even *irrelevant* to the problem at hand? Not at hand *at present*, he knows well enough at present to be sure, but previously so, and in a larger hand than his is...than he has ever thought *his* hand to be...

φ

He thinks within an atmosphere that's framed by that inertia, the initial disappointment that spurred him towards this goal. A search for the return to where he always has... he always *must* return to, for reasons that he cares not to return to at the moment, but that he makes a note to take the time to note again. He sees himself within the tribulations and gratuities of an adventure whose conclusion is quite tragic, and already long resolved, but such emergent circumstance—while fixed by that first impulse—is only conjoined *to it* by some dithering proximity, some arbitrary kinship to its middle term...

φ

Perhaps someday he'll understand the whole of what compels him as that stamp of narrativity *set up* by start and end; perhaps he'll soon consider every step that's happened to him since he first began this plummet as an apologue, a fable from which generations forward to the eschaton can learn some prudent lesson that within it he can't limn. What concerns him now is none of this...this postured importunity; what matters is that he maintain the limits of his standing, whatever it turns out those limits yet turn out to be...

φ

It may be true that if he ever hits his haunt again he'll find that it's abandoned by the others...those others still made servant to the cruelty of such rigid strand. If he ever finds that reference point—that frame in which to grieve—then he may well be freed of it—*possess* it, so be freed of understanding it a possible possession—but this is not the gist of his assignment *or* his plight. He's accepted that for him there is no promised comfort; it's how this coddled divagation started, way back when. He finds no subtle pleasure in the forfeit that first pushed him towards this inferential target, to let himself fall forward in accordance with this dream, but rather it's the sense of some still dilating disquiet that drives him to attempt an understanding of his status, the affliction he's abidingly ensnared himself within. It's not that this insensate inclination—or *grade* of inclinations, brought together by some common aim—is not marshalled…is not *focused* in accordance with his needs and satisfactions, but that the best he ever hopes for—that he has ever *gotten*, so to fix it as proof—is avoidance of the furthering debasement of his station; the *maintenance* of what little he's got left…

φ

Perhaps it's better thought, he thinks, as something like the endless…the endlessly protracting supplication of his posture to what he still imagines as its future lowest point. He wants but to retard it, that intractable declension, not because he wouldn't do more—stop it outright *by reversing*—but for the certainty he's given up all hope of doing more by predilection, by *desire*—all hope in what such wanting *does* by merely want itself. If *he*, that is to say, that is as he and he alone…if he is to *effect* some next persuasive termination, however it's observably confirmed as such a stall, then it's sure to have required a coincident conformity to what he thinks amounts to the constraints of *every* finish, every…

φ

Of course he knows quite well that there are many other options, that there *have been* on the way to where he finds himself right now, but that bears no relation to his thinking his path over—to conceiving of another end, another hapless goal. He has no one result he's going after, has not trained his eye to pull some static target from the viscid null, and this not for the regimen he's only just expounded—that of following such paradigm over what he merely *thinks* he wants—but from his own indifference to the standard of its discharge, his apathy to *every* path when forced to think

self-interest cause for making such a choice. He does not care, he tells himself, what blank he turns his gaze towards, nor what aspect of that vision can resolve him to the view, so much as that he follows that first principle he's come to...that he *asserts* he's come to, regardless if he has done, or if he's only mentioned it in passing, as a child's ruse; that principle being—that state of grace, of perfect grace, requiring...

φ

He's certain that he's thought of it, he's thought of it before; he *associates* its former derivation with some portion of his present view, but not only that, not only that...he's sure that it's not only that, that there was there before there, something there before...

φ

He's sure that he has landed on this principle too often... much too often to allow himself to think only of *this* time, this *particular* delay. He understands that when he asks himself the question—when he poses his repose as such an inward abdication to an outward dray—he responds with what he thinks can't be accounted any anything—not even any *nothing*—an amorphous sensitivity to some pain having happened before this static turn. Before this present syncope, before he was *this* person; if only he could understand...could *calculate* the principle as incident...as *principle*...

φ

It's this, he now recalls, that he's forgotten to remember, that he could somehow hope to soon forget it ever more.

This fact of his eliding what he knows he'll rediscover…
what he'll haul up from the deepest depths, as though to
bring the ceiling to the floor…He knows that what persuaded him to walk this motile border is that he'd left out
something…something—and he can't remember what.
That he can't remember what he can't remember—what
he couldn't at the moment that he *tried* to, on a lark—is but
another act of evidentiary surrender to the impulse, which
to him seems quite enough to restore his faith…his faith
in…It surprises him, he thinks again, that he has faith in
anything, that he has ever had such faith in anything at all.
Perhaps this is the bit of luck he's long been trailing after,
the outside of the inside that will show him—will *illumi-
nate*—his future path, both where he's been and…

φ

Another hapless circumnavigation of the problem he's
been trying for some time to get across, to make more
plain…the problem with continuing in the first place, contrived the vagrant cipher that sets up the nearing next in
line. He's not only been somewhere…*many* places disregarded as he placed himself among them; not only does
he travel towards some cursory accession to the *habitus* of
being in again; but he is also in position…in a system that
he knows he can't maintain himself atop, no less within…

φ

Not that he would want to if he could; there's little that's
compelling him to action, but for the absent obverse, the
consequence of ever doing…ever *thinking* otherwise a rational pursuit. Now that he's *here* there's nothing better…he
can think of nothing better than maintaining his predicament until he's got a plan—an *outside* to transpose against

his viscera, his nner brume. It's not worth much, he understands, he hasn't found his purpose—or the absence of his purpose—in this exuberant polemic, but…

φ

His faith is in the moment, in the portent of the moment, as he seizes it in verity—then gist. Of course he knows the way…the *many* ways his grueling transit as *and into* such a passing thing—a thing lived in the passing—has led him to this abject perspicacity…this *presence* in the inverse pose it seems he's living now. He knows that he has passed through other chances, that he's attained this standing by the weight of many smaller acts—acts that led him to this place…this placement in this place…that led him only *here*, that is, to here and here alone. What those actions were, and in whose name he has performed them…what the scheme by which he's entered *this* menace is unclear, and for all his vain desire to expose those signal causes he believes that such discovery would not…*need* not soon or ever yield the benefice of egress, of passage to the comforts of a stable mien. Which is what he wants, he thinks, in the midst of all these concerts and amusements, if not everything he's *ever* thought a possible…

φ

That he has reached his present state by some impassioned culling of conditions and responses to conditions—a willful syncopation of desires and *fulfillments* of desires with the circumstance that manifests the same—is not itself a method to make manifest…to *articulate* what those conditions have been…what either those conditions or the choices laid out by them ever have been or are now. He thinks that he has understood his present situation, and with such grand discernment has identified his standing in relation to his purchase, as unlikely as that is to soon produce a craved result. And so each fleet decision that he finds himself awakening...for which he is *responsible*, as though he were the agent of some preternatural prime, he comes to think...to think *again* the new frame that he's placed in — that he's placed *himself* within, and not beyond...

φ

Every choice amounts to a reduction of first causes to their seconds...is subsequent to making it...*by* making it made so fully indifferent to its maker that such a one can find no way to make it out again. Once he's made his choice, he comes to realize he can't realize what he's done without including in his realization every sequence...every measure of *inconsequence* correspondingly performed. The problem is he hasn't rid himself of that autonomy...that presumed *condition* of autonomy that prodded his surrender to this bloodless stour; can't properly absorb his hard won knowledge of his own discrete irrelevance in a way that would prevent him from believing the next seizure of the next attempt *to strive* will result in something other than the same loss of persistency, of a world construed as static — the same that he's been suffering through...

φ

He thinks he's proved the vigor of his own inert kinesis — of his presence as a mover — well beyond the steady murmur of this bland incomprehension, though whether he has ever done...has ever tried...but no. He remembers this one act — this one *emprise* — of remonstration; that everything he does involves an infinite protraction of inscrutable events which he has plausibly made happen — which are as much of personed will as of engendered purpose—within which nothing can be understood the smallest part...

φ

Every step needs balance for the next step to move forward; one may make one's wishes known—one may well *express* them—by inclining towards some point in space, thus proffering some otherwise intrinsic destination as an end, but what one does to get there—what one stomachs for *fulfillment*—can't include all that one does to manage that comportment; every footstep after footstep, every wheezing, shallow gasp...

φ

He's mapped this ground in ways he feels need no further repeating, a claim already proven by arriving here—at any here—at any time at all. The reason he still brings it up, now that it's indisputable, is that by doing so he has succeeded in returning...in *winning a way back* to where he was...to where *he would be* if he'd been there all along. Yes, he does so many things to make his doings possible—to make what he thinks possible a possible result—that he can't hope to count them—to think each one discernible—even if forever more he should refuse to stop; he still recounts the difference between things he doesn't know he's done until they are thus counted and those that—in the midst of such—he need only recall to know they're his...

φ

He is presently reminded—he reminds *himself*, at least—that in coming to invert what he had thought of as proportion— what he thought would be his touchstone of proportion *in the past*—he's developed needs he would not have had he been more assertive in progressing towards the end for which he started starting out. For which he started forward in the name of this misgiving—whose name, that is to say, he hasn't had the mind to speak. He has made himself conversant with so many frames of reference, frames in which he had no notion that he'd been immersed, that coming back to even this awareness of confusion—of the form of his disjointed persecution of all forms—seems a kind of progress, a progress against regress to the next progressive action—action in the service of an ever shifting final cause...

φ

Perhaps this situation isn't one that would inspire such conviction to *break out* within the churl of lumpen leisure who meanders quickly past...quickly *through*, if he can help it, which he can in this dictation even if he still can't know it... think it...*admit* it to himself; such undue presentiment seems to him at worst a nuisance, at best another catalyst to pursue it next time round, a method of asserting he's unlikely to make those mistakes so common to his peerage, that he will not *repeat* the wrongs that captivate the ire of his many witless rants. Oh, he's had his chances, he's aware of their gestation, as a swarm that builds its rancid hive within his throbbing pate. Yes, he could stand up, he could run forward that same instant, in the instant of his waking he could go right back to sleep, but what good would that do, why at *this* point would such regress from the mission of his missionary canon appear anything but tangent, but distraction from the stasis he's persuaded is the goal. At least it's his, he tells himself, it still belongs to him...

φ

At least it is his own, he thinks, it's within his possession, admitting that some other could advance it just as well. He doesn't care—and doesn't know—if his position can be claimed the leaping farrow of another backwards and intrepid cur, but more importantly than either his subjunction or his subtlety, he has no present notion what the difference is...what the difference *would be* if it were *his* fate. To be as much the given of another as his own, as he is as his own...

φ

Perhaps put in the path of that irrational alterity his pose would be instructive, or possibly the waste of yet another afternoon, but even though he finds the prospect genial, if not curious—of some *implicit* interest—he has no idea how he would trace his passage to it, how he could ever find it out, if it is in fact still in. For all intents and purposes—all purposes conceived of as forthcoming and persistent—the posture that he's taken is his own, and only that, and...

φ

And if he is alone then he alone has had his chances, he alone has chosen *this* course by avoiding every chance... has avoided every chance to choose another...another *sort* of ending; to amble vainly forward without concern for fate or pitch—this, he thinks, is all that differentiates *his* passion from other transitory sufferings, those so many others would abide if they were pressed to the acceptance of such salutary rut. What distinguishes such strain from every other advent—every that he *could* pursue, assuming his odd bent—is that his choices are determined by admitting his fatality, and not by any obstinate attempt to root out some forthcoming suffering, to clear a pathway *to deliverance*...

φ

One need not understand one's fate as some form of deliverance—as a terminus beyond all sense of personage or
state. It is a *tempting* error, he more than merely fancies—a
fallacy, he thinks, that he's deferred to in the past—but such
thought doesn't mean he can say when, or what, or…

φ

Most significant to him is that he's forsworn the ambition to
seek comfort in a practice whose nativity is fixed in an *intuitive* dismissal of the slope he's traveled to the cleft he's in. Of
what is here and now, that is, what's happening right now
right when it's happening and not after it's been understood
as central to his history…to his elided history, a moment
when the history of histories is erased…He's able to discern—he has been at it for some time now—that there is no
significance to what one gives significance, that what seems
most important to one's prosecuted purpose is a manner of
recusancy, of taking back the meaning of what means most
in the present, in the present of the future just as likely…

φ

The present of the future is as much a present reference to
the future future's past as it is presently referred to as the
portent of the present, as it functions to divert one from the
sense of present portent…

φ

It is tempting, he remembers—he's been tempted in the
past—and even now…He's always found it tempting to
look forward to the future as if there were *no* present, as if

one's pithy boding of a formulated plan resolves into fruition only then, and he has had his chances to repent that futile seizure of the motive, of the ending of all endings as his cause, if not his aim, but such is not...such decision *would not be* consistent with his nature, with what he finds he can't control...*deter* of his disinclination to pursue what that pursuit obliges every actor to ignore—all active denotation and distinction in the moment, all trace of coming to the meaning of a present future term...

φ

It's possible for one to make an argument against this form of agency, this prodigal disdain, accepting that pursuit of future triumphs and incursions is born not from desire to achieve the next conclusion, but from the need to ignore *this* one, the fear of what's in store should one accept one's present frame...

φ

To be the stable referent to which every near abstraction serves as gesture still requires that the knower not aspire to make action out of movement, to consider such immersion in the moment as abandonment of every hope...of every thought of concord or refrain. Knowing what he knows— and knowing that he knows it—means he can't conceive of doing any else or aft, and as such every *this* he might have understood as purpose in conclusion stands before him as immersive scan. That every fate he's ever to have suffered is at present...is *immediate*...

φ

In this sense, he imagines, he no longer has such chances, he can no longer consider his position as a choice. It's not that he believes there weren't other opportunities—that there haven't been in traveling to meet *this* fulsome post—but that he thinks his modus in deciding between pathways is by reference to substance, not causation; not to purpose, but...

φ

He chooses in each instant that he's cognizant of choices what he's able to determine...to *distinguish* as the most nearly sufficient to the prospect of some more or less discernible—which is to say efficient—liberation from all sense of having finished...His deficiency of purpose is not only problematic in the broad view, but writ upon the minimal diversity of form installed before him, that awaits him every time he looks up from his...from the pose of his poltroonery, to take it in...What he chooses is awareness, is to need what he receives as a receiver of the world—what he's given without any first reflection, or a second...

φ

He's chosen not to supplement his sense of what's *at present* with the frittering distractions of imagined worlds to come, and so he thinks *his* choice was not quite ever such an option—not a choice or a desire, not a verdict or a vote—but amounts to an accession to necessity, to what he thinks is manifestly, evidently so. The evidently *true*, he thinks, may be ignored with pleasure—may be shuttled front and sideways to accommodate a ready aim—but it will be no less true for that willful supplication, and one will always find one's way back to it in the end...

φ

But even this assertion renders his imperious surrender to conclusion as a choice, if not quite chosen, and such disdainful haze is what he'd like to here—if only here—avoid, or move beyond. He does not want to fall into the ocean of delusion by which he'd take the next step to conceal a truth that only he has cordoned...that only he shows to himself, if not another...

φ

He wants to make his point, and so he comes to it directly; he thinks it fair to call this indecision an accomplishment that only he alone has chosen—that he alone has chosen *once again*—but that's the only thing...the only *moment of decision* he can think of...he can grasp as it flits by, if not take in...

φ

All this, he understands, has nothing much to do with it. If it were indeed his choice—a choice he'd just as likely choose to think was something...was *anything* but—then perhaps the way he feels would have some relevance to something...to something...What he means, rather—what he'd like to *demonstrate* he meant, whether he means it now or not—is that no matter what his preference or preferment it is simply not the truth as he's received it—as it's *manifest*—thus he can't be said to choose it, contrary to his antecedent claims. He may not remain faithful to experience or reason, which to him are always moving towards agreement, thus allied, but whatever he does next—what pose he takes in any precinct—he can't escape the truth... the very truth of...

φ

What draws him to the margins—to the whimsy of his limit—is always irrefutably his immediate predicament, itself the certain nature of his naturing of purpose in the world. It's not that he can't estimate his many disparate options, what seem to him his choices in each scene as it drifts by— each bracket of the temporal that's posited as present, a present that endures until it cedes to its next final iteration...

φ

He knows that he has choices, their character aside, but he also understands the verge that binds them to his system— that structures their discernment—is found in the attention that makes possible the culling of sensation from the infinite extension of all one could *conceivably* derive. He knows that he is torn—like every self he can imagine—between feeling and surveillance, that what he feels is still an act of scrutiny—an oscillation of his scrutiny to engage an inner brink—and as such he's incapable of thinking of his role in the continuance of living... his life limned in his living it as anything but following each necessity to the next one, and the next...

φ

Yes, there are those moments when he'd rather just continue, when he can't imagine keeping up this standard or this pace, but he notices too much of what's been...of what's *going on* about him to allow for that contingency to take up time or amplitude, to let concern for motive have an influence on how he remains fixed in this conciliated place. He's pacified his place, he thinks, it seems a near necessity...

φ

It may assume the form of a necessity, but evidence of finding any prospect of its obverse...of its *opposite* an internal negation of the same is still unthinkable, if not quite thought unthought. So what precisely does it mean to claim this intervention an activity of following along—of making *progress*—without even the *chance* of doing otherwise, a passage that was always *firstly* taken as a duty, an implicit debt? Does he really find his present state, whatever it may be...has he *ever found* his enterprise a peon to necessity? Is it true that one cannot conceive of any purpose otherwise—that *he* cannot conceive of it while in such dire perch? Of any purpose otherwise compelled at his behest...

φ

And if he can't conceive of it—he knows this of his nature—then neither can another, not any other similarly limited in means. *His* means, that is to say—the means of reason, pure and simple—are not rebutted or established by what they pivot *on*, what act of dreamed malfeasance or vituperative delay. It seems to him the primacy...the *substance* of necessity—that one can't think it otherwise, or if one does it's only due to some kind of mistake. There are those who've reasoned poorly—he hasn't always been exempt—not knowing as they do so what that competence evokes, but their mistakes cannot be claimed as *attributes* of reason; they serve as the peculiar supervenience of circumstance made orderly by easy confutation...by the ease of such purveyors in that sump of confutations, no matter if they jumped in—or were thrown...

φ

Alas, this binding premise of confirmed noncontradiction—not only in experience, but intrinsic to the thingness

of the thing, set in itself—does not seem apropos of his relinquished status...the status he's apparently relinquished
himself *to*. Would it not be possible for him to have done
otherwise? That this world—as it's granted him and as
he acts within it—should never have been what it is, the
same as it appears? Is there warrant to believe that his submission to that commonweal could not have brought him
elsewhere? That he couldn't have been other and still be as
himself? Or come to live an otherwise by remaining as he
has been, as he is soon to think...to *know* himself to be? Is
there any sense to claiming...to *believing* that without some
heap of arbitrary predicates assigned to dwindling subject
such a subject would be forfeit to another host and footing, would never be conceived of...be *conceivable* in the first
place, wherever that may be, or be received...

φ

The dilemma, he well knows, is not an easy one to settle;
he's hit again upon the shoals of this presumptive shore.
And even if he isn't so much comfortable with the metaphor—with *any* metaphor, that is, for grounds he cares not
to elaborate, so to tell himself before he meets the exigence
that prods him towards his present end...Whatever that is.
Whatever end will end his *present* present as the driver of
the ends that drive him presently...

φ

He knows that this new quandary is not one he'll likely
overcome—that he'll ever likely overcome—but that hasn't
yet deterred him from confronting what confronts him, or
allowed him to eschew any distraction from his sense of its
essential...its *substantive*—if not *quite* essential—pause. He
thinks of doing otherwise—everything and anything from

some positing of indolence fixed otherwise, or *out*—and this is the objective that inspires him to waver in the face of his exception...what he thinks is his exception from the nature of his kind. Which is...

φ

If he can but envision doing what he has decided...what he's chosen not to *do* as much to say, then what does it mean that he should steer so surely towards redemption, towards *fulfillment* in finale—his attainment of cessation in display? That he should meet his vision of pursuable... of *reasonably* pursued pursuits by deducing the necessity of pursuing them, that is, when it's within his stupefied capacity to think the thing—the thingness of his object in the world—in an infinite variety of other ways? An infinite that still proclaims an outside...

φ

He can imagine, after all, his going forward with a discourse on the premise of a preference that he's only just expressed—his preference for ignoring his preference to ignore any discussion of his preference—a fact of plausibility made evident *as* fact by his endeavors to dissuade himself from doing so; the fulfillment of his need to turn away from his desire by explaining to himself his desire is to turn away from his desire...He often has—is often *possessed by*—contradictory aims, whether he has them or not, which one would think precludes the attribution of necessity to his motives *or* his choices; which one might *presume*, that is to say, would keep him from attributing necessity to his attribution of necessity to...

φ

One might imagine that along with his desire to convince…
to convince *himself* of the fatality of his chosen course, so of
the illusory attachment of a motive to the appearance of his
purpose in the world…that within that very act of making
truth claims on behalf of what he thinks of as a life he could
not *not* live—that he had no choice *but* assent to, free and
clear—is implicit an acceptance that he could have chosen
something else, that he could still…

φ

There is a sense, he long ago presumed himself to realize—before this awkward tonnage first began to draw
him down—in which his present argument works as well
for any other faculty of virtue—of *prepotency*; that his
choices are not only necessary predicates of some govern-
able nature—such as his is, if it's sure of his alone—but
are evidence of what that fecund faculty can come to when
it's turned upon one's ordinary comportment in the world.
That what he is attempting to confirm is *not* his nature, so
much as it's his nature to pursue…

φ

That he knows that he knows something he doesn't know
as gnosis—a quantity numerically identical to the volume
of the reservoir he knows as full awareness…as full *knowledge* of his knowing self—is an inner corollary to such
fungible awareness of the outside, a stockpile he draws
from…that he *uses*, if unwittingly…He discerns within
himself the need to posit an alterity that's nonetheless still
his and his alone, but only given the impulsion—the indeterminate *multiplicity*—of his variable moieties, his incon-
clusive catalogue of conclusive bounds. That he is thus
alone himself—distinct from every other slipshod harmony

of rendered modes—still doesn't mean he's singular...

φ

There is no other way, he thinks, to think his inner sense
of knowing homogeneous with what his knowing in the
instant of his knowing it implies—no other way but to
allege an inner that gives sanction to that knowledge that
one uses while not knowing that one knows it, that such
usance names a corollary plan...

φ

He's not only sought a method for describing the mechanics
by which he uses uses without knowing they're employed,
but so doing he's revealed that every other figure of the
thing within its thingness—unrelated to its status as an inside or an out—must establish the deferral of its issue—of
all completed purpose—from what's settled into some yet
indiscernible account. His sense of himself sensing—of his
actions in accordance with some knowable...some *singular*
design—avers, he thinks, an inner by which such fractured
praxis is surmounted...is an implemented personhood...
means that there are meanings that he doesn't know he's
meaning and despite such revelation never once divulged
them, nor traveled towards...

φ

And similarly, he'll never know—*no one*, that is to say, will
ever know—the full extent of what he...what such a one
as he can know as knowing, the breach of being other than
himself. He may realize he can't realize the abundance
of his mandates—so he has, if it's uncertain, if he hasn't
yet again; he may still learn the methods he's employed to

know his defects—the plurality of purpose that propels him through this ruled disdain—but he can't know them fully… know them *wholly*, as an end, because within each purport of a practicable absence there are infinite divergencies, if not varieties of divergence…

φ

If it's possible to know more than what he knows he knows at present, if he can *project* the image of an intellect so capacious that from his lowly purview it appears another infinite expression of a finite stretch, then it must be the case that no such personage as he is…as they are…as one could ever hope to be could know its horde of gnosis to completion, an avowal he can no longer deny the name necessity…

φ

It's required in all instances of being in the world—of being as a being that receives itself as sensate, as an outer that sees inner as its purpose, as its aim—that there are things one knows that are not known as known at present—that are knowable, perhaps, but are not rightly thought known now. That something is not knowable he can well understand; that knowing what's unknowable is still a knowing form, a form of know-how…

φ

What concerns him, once again, is not this awkward stature— the anguish at remaining so confused, without a scheme— so much as its necessity, the inexorable mote in which he's seemingly imprisoned—the runnel which he's lastingly… *eternally* immured himself within. And this, as well, not for the cherished *sense* of such deduction but just that it seems possible, that it's happened, here and there; that it's even once been possible to postulate necessity not verified... not *tested* by appealing to its internal consistency — by the benchmark of some fatuous consistency alone. There are some types of necessity that amount to countermanding any two opposing predicates in one objective form, but there are others that in concept make that alternate seem possible... *prove* that any deviation contradicts the mode from which that causal *mise-en-scene* declines...

φ

All this for some purpose he remembers...he remembers as...He thinks that it's important to discriminate necessity in what appears an otherwise contingent aftermath because it means that what he means...that what he meant by granting such necessity to what emerged a wholly arbitrary...an *aleatory* choice...He concedes, that is, that what he means was always arrayed other than what he believed he meant just then, which was...

φ

He's had enough of this confusion, he would like to now move on. And so in lithe accord with this facsimile of wanting — this likeness of his liking to the world he's left behind — he must turn back to that return on which his next turn hinges, return to that last turn on which his world turns now he's in it...

φ

He hopes to be in this world where formerly he'd left it — that's the lesson, he's aware, but he's sure that its expression isn't clear. He's never seen a way out, as if he had been looking; he's never *sought* an out for knowing that he'd never find it, notwithstanding how impressive his endeavors have become. That the *in* he's in has given itself over to some steady state he might have thought an out if he had only thought it present, which is always the right moment to...

φ

He knows that where he is is from the outside not quite affect, that he's more than merely *occupied* this scrupulous repose. There's always been more to it than some posture or expression; his thinking on the nature of his thinking... of his thinking and his posture both are just as much a parcel...part and parcel of his placement, the construction of his present *in*, and so his outward view. There is a difference, he remembers—or thinks he thinks he knows—between the realm he shares with others living in it, and the mirror of the dissonance that opens to...

φ

It's possible, he thinks, to parse the feckless life he's living between that which he knows others know and what he knows himself...*inside* himself, a space he shares with no one...that he *wants* to share with no one—thus a difference in his purview, not his nature or his type. Both states ascertained by this emergent deprivation are constructed as perspectives, and must finally conform to the same rules in this regard. Both the inside and the outside are made object by and with the cardinal seer for whom inside meets its out, that is, and so...

φ

183

All this to say his purpose in defining his position at *this* moment, refusing to discern its faintly designated presence a distinction in anything but form...his purpose here has nothing much to do with a return to his awareness of location or arrangement—which he has never left, as far as he's concerned—but instead returns him to remembrance of that moment of transition that defined his present course. He is on a course that could branch off in an instant, and as it could, he understands, it has done and will soon. In this sense, every moment is distinguished as a turning, every unknowing persistency an action to avoid the change as it admits each present role, the change in state that every inclination thus includes...He knows, that is, that every course is made up...is *constructed* of a gala pullulation of such incidental turnings, and there's little to distinguish one such hinge of apposition from the next in line...

φ

Little, but not nothing, he repeats with hopeful pride; little is not nothing, and for this he feels a gratitude he can't fully accommodate, nor otherwise avoid—that he can't find a method of avoiding...There is little that distinguishes one critical divergence from the differential parsing of such corollary turns, but little is more than nothing, he repeats, and more than nothing is sufficient...is sufficient to...

φ

One thinks, he thinks, the crux that one returns to as a purpose...as an *exploit* that the present either has or will fulfill by seeing such a presence as itself a realization of some turning that *might* happen...might have happened in an instant, or an eon still...It is possible, that is, to make distinctions of importance—of varying importance to one's picture of the scene—by deciding...by *gleaning* from that vantage what's important to one's standing, and so to the position that one hopes to hold, to come to hold...One must determine what it is one *wants* to target, what of the many ends one is persistently pursuing one wants most to mete the future, far or near, near or...

φ

It seems an easy inference, now that he's thought to think it, but that doesn't make achieving it any easier at all; it makes such an achievement appear possible—even *abeyant*—which may indeed be measurably easier than its obverse, but that doesn't mean it's easy, nor confer a sense of ease to its pursuit...

φ

He does not really want...does not *know how* to want to make a move towards any anything...towards any *other* anything distinguished as an end...But this, he soon accepts—this *stasis* in the midst of ineluctable resolve—is an action in the service of conclusion, of a terminus; of some purpose only realized after it's been thought complete. He is doing what he's doing—he is always doing something—whether he likes it...whether he *wants* to be as nothing...*to be nothing* in the service of his doing, that is to say, or not...

φ

He may not want to make a move, to start a new progression, but he has done, he can't help it, so he might as well apply himself to what makes him contented, what sustains the vacant promise of returning him to ease of mind and mood. This might be a far sight more than he can really come to; there might be nothing left for him to assay and achieve; but *if* there's nothing left—so no option is presented—then it seems to him he might as well embrace it, as a choice...

φ

If he's going to do something, then he's well resolved to make the doing *of* it follow principle, to find himself back at his goal by looking out...by looking towards and into...

φ

By looking towards conclusion he feels certain he'll soon find another way of looking back, which is all he really wants, he thinks, what he's trying to accomplish...He's looking for a way to look back into...into what first brought him here, as though to fill its pliant frame, and by that vision turn himself against...

φ

By showing up the means through which his future is ascendant—is ascending towards the present with the bearing of a gain—he wants to bring back what he's always left behind in transit, what he requires to return to his indelible attention—turn his next attention *towards*—if so he hopes to move in the direction of release from this daft penchant for release, for the last...

φ

There was some time not long ago—some fulcrum of ambition—when he first located the bound between himself and his accumulated predicates, and at that breakneck detour from implicit to discovered he remorselessly contrived his brink—and all his world—revolted; he had the supreme insight his perspective was inverse. Not upside down, he thinks—his measly measure of redundancy—but from the out to in, the in to out...

φ

Again his primal cognizance of what marks off...*divides* the mucid fields within him from the fringe that mews the outside...of seeing that the fringe that marks the pull of the extrinsic as the limit of his dissonant velleity, that is, is that he has received it, that he takes it as the object of his perorating spew. That he limns it—that he *knows* it—proves it is as such without him, even though it seems within his taciturn control, and that he now luxuriates in the muck of his discretions means that everything that shares that place is predicate, thus known. One must be as a vector gleaning oneness from array, must always push back pushing back by pushing always into; must ever push back into...

φ

A necessity, he understands, that even his deduction of necessity can't manage to forestall. And that, he's almost certain, was the object he was aiming towards, and his reaching it provides him with a moment to trace footfalls that would otherwise be covered by the molder of an autumn gale. What grandiloquence, he thinks, what florid wit flows from his failures and his victories alike; how easy to accept a trope that's drafted in the employ of some potency—some *proven* strength—accepted as confessed. But this, too, is not his mission or his purpose; that any surely incidental following of tangent—any subtle divagation from this promise of return—will take him where

187

he's never been, which in this instant…in this *particular* instant must always be an elsewhere he is anxious to elude…

φ

It's easy to make light of what one suffers by presuming the attraction of the beautiful a *justified* deceit. In this case, the duplicity would be obvious to *any* acumen on guard against what might be thought a sanable mistake; he has not yet revealed his maiden purpose or objective—that unresolved ambition towards which he started out—by following his vestiges…by *tracing his path backwards* to the source, but he's achieved those same results by doing only otherwise, by traveling in circles; he has come back to the juncture where he first sheered from his system by continuing to swerve from any symbol…any *sign* of its resumption—from any and all inkling of its coming into view…

φ

The problem that he has with this improbable conclusion is not that it inveighs against some chosen…some merely *preferable* course, but that it doesn't yield to an associated principle, that it has not thereby…there*to* yielded, and as such it appears a deleterious…an *unusable* result. He cannot say, he realizes—and none too soon at that—that he should take this one case of indenture to the tangent for a rule with which he must comply if he's to come to any point by any means again. Why, even here, even now… even *this* attempt at seizure—at the seizing of this moment as though it were his last—would be a failure if continued, if continued without…

φ

He feels that if he can't stop stopping each and every next attempt at such compelled pursuit it stands to reason he won't have the reason to pursue it, nor find the means to find the means to any sure result. And more than that, it follows, if there is no real distinction—no sustainable dispute—between the claim of gainful purpose and some random...some *arbitrary* following of impulse in the name of easy choice, then there is no justification for seeking out a terminus, and the argument for following—adduced *against* such progress—can be dismissed in principle *and* effect...

φ

Let us say one understands conducting some digression—abandoned to the urgency or languor of the need—a method to give meaning to one's journey...to one's *pathway*; what, he wants to know, can one envision as the augur thereby gratified, the fatality thus sanctioned, thus *attained*? What the consequence of thinking some desired target—itself still triggered accidentally—as though it were fulfillment of the principle of always acting counter to fulfillment, against all means to prosecute such discernible intent? The principle of acting against every active principle...

φ

If nothing else, he reasons, is it not always imaginable... can one not always imagine some plan drawn from knowing guess both as target and excursus worth pursuing to its finish? What can such a scattered mind conjecture as conclusion, as conclusory in any time, this one or the next? Is there not in every origin that's ever thought effectively the cause of such portentous ends an endless train of purposes, of aims that one *could* trace across all future bearing out? Does one not need to make the choice between two paths discerned in temporal coincidence, even if that choice should be accomplished by obeisance to chance? And this particular instance of return to foregone purpose—while occasioned by genteel perseveration in its way—was evidenced...was evidently *unconcealed* by imputation of result to such a following of tangent, and equally rejecting what's occurred to him...all that's since occurred to him as...

φ

He may find his way back to where he set out—he *departed*—but he won't do so in a manner he can generalize to any other instance of return to meet his path; he may scamper in circles while coercing some improvement... some *illusory* advancement from the wind that whips the precincts of his unprotected face, but whatever else results from such conclusive anabasis every principle to drive his future course still rests *behind* him, and so remains forever beyond his grasp...

φ

What his divagations prove is that he's chosen them from many...from *countless* other options that are fixed within his glance, the illimitable aggregation he's failed to excise from his boundless task. The infinite beside him is still equal in all measure to that infinite he banishes within... that void which, looking inward, he instantiates as outside, as marking off an *inner* out, an inner bounding line. He's inside as he's outside, as he's inside just the same, but that inside is external to his warrant—is still *outside*—insofar as he can place it, as it's been discerned...

φ

Thus there is necessity implied by chains of circumstance—circumstances thought as a coincidence of unrelated terms—when closer analysis—closer to replete *examination*—shows that nothing else is possible...*was* possible, in image *or* in act. This, he understands, is the position that he takes in all his choices and diversions, all his principles in principle and translated to force; this is what provokes him, even though... even *when* he doesn't know it, such instances, it may well be, as haven't settled out, or happened yet...

φ

He understands that looking back to what he's looking back to—in looking back to what he thinks he's able *to accept*—he ascertains no way of choosing other than he's chosen; his choices, such as they appear, could not have been made otherwise, were culled from the fortuitous convergence of futilities by following the lines already drawn...

φ

To understand his choices are not yet precisely chosen, are always chosen for him—always by him and thus for him, before they meet his wont—is not a way of coding fate into his guiding doctrine, of making his advancement an indenture to exemption—to anything, that is to say, *but* choice...

φ

He asks no further proof that freedom always needs necessity, that any choice is chosen from the prospect of some stance; from choices thought as possible to choose from—to *distinguish*—regardless of the sundry means by which one stumbles down but one of all such possible paths. It makes no sense to choose what one is sure can never happen, to make a choice that's proven inconceivable first off. If it did, then he would do so, he would do it without question, and run to meet a grander fate, a flea to bound and skip among the stars...

φ

He can dream, it seems to him, of still quite disparate chances, chances he may not have now but in some time to come...and this itself seems warrant to consider such analysis as not completely realized—not in any sense confutative or determinant or done. The fact that one can image situations that can't happen—that never have, that *couldn't* have, which amounts to the same claim—is understood as evidence of freedom...

φ

He's made a common plaint of his desire to be somewhere that is ever not the where he's ever been, to find himself discharged into some post of greater stature than his present outlook seems, and to that end he long ago began this declination, to countervail what's led him to this overwhelming pull, a pose whose aimed debasement can't be qualified, which is again...again to say...

φ

It seems that his attempts to rectify his station—to make his life, and so the living of it, somehow *else*—implies that his advancement is uncertain, that it has not been determined, thus continues to proscribe the gathered sooth of making choices...

φ

For all his restless claims to living in and through necessity, he believes that what's to come is only actualized by choosing, by the newness of new choices, and the chance he has within his permeable bracket to *make present* his next purchase, so to purchase his next suppliance to fate. He believes that he has choices—he has never once denied it—and that making them determines what will happen...what will come into his purview as direction—as *result*—but when he brings his choosing to the same consideration he's applied to his analysis of plausible alternatives—to the malady that opens his discernment of his varied next—he sees that what impels him into this or that decision—what determines what he chooses in the moment that he makes the choice—is no more tenably interior than what goes on about him; is only his surrender to an inner chosen for him...given *to* him, as a *necessary* state...

φ

He has his inclinations, his desires and his wants, and they are no more chosen by him—even as he picks *among* them—than the dossier of everything he thinks of as a possible effect...He's no more able to manipulate his protean velleities than he can change the nature of the world in which he's thrust, the world in which he acts against all patent disposition...

φ

This, he thinks, is surely worth pursuing for a moment; as though such worth—or its negation—has proved motive in the past. Of course he doesn't think that it will *someday* be worth something, but that *it is* and on such grounds anoints it with the thrill of his ingenuous pursuit. In those jaunts that seemed fruitful but that now appear abortive, he pursued them thinking otherwise, that they might soon produce some sort of measurable growth—soon enough, that is, to be mistaken in that fancy, his allotment...

φ

It occurs to him that even this odd maunder into affect—if that's really what it is, if it's ever once resulted in some palpable impact—was not quite chosen...not *considered*, even, for the greatness of its value; he didn't just *decide* to persevere in this surmise of his pursuit of value because he thought it valuable...

φ

To be honest, he continues, as though he could imagine any purpose in the lie...To be *candid* he had not discerned the value of pursuing such a course before he chose it—before he noticed choosing it, the *it* that now permits him these constitutive delays. He was not aware of choosing it, even as he chose it; he could have chosen otherwise, but he didn't think it even for a moment before doing so—before choosing to do what he's done *in defiance* of its worth. He believes that it's worth something, that moving towards this end has given something to him he'd otherwise have been denied, but what that is...what that that is...what that that is is...

φ

An infinite regress of receivable results forms the substrate of discernment—the *nature* of considering one's place within the world—and so is the arcane consideration of his prospects—of the prospect of his choosing between prospects—subject to the same regressive standard that invigorates all other professed knowledge into act. It is surely no great enterprise of deduction—or even evidence of his skills in this regard—to say some one occasion prompts the turning out of every other...*makes way* for what one's tumble into *future* term will be. It is not novel to consider that one's choices are determined...are made semblant in the world by forces that *appear* to have had nothing much to do with choice, to do with choosing; that seem to every subject who receives them to constrict...

φ

But his insight is not found in this tumescence of profundity—this vain attempt to make the most quotidian of rules appear the *clef* of his *roman*; instead, it comes in realizing the world's not fixed around him, not made outside by becoming...by *embodying* conditions over which he still has little...he has *no* control, that is; in *accepting* that his sensing of particulars is what succors his alterity, the dynamic alms of notice that makes *sense* of the infinity outside him, just as well as closed within...

φ

As though discretion were a predicate of the thing—the very *object*—thus distinguished as discernibly discrete. There is a sense in which one can achieve some least assurance of the certainty at rest within one's dilating awareness by remembering that one neither creates it nor controls it, does not turn one's notice to it in a manner that allows one to attempt to turn it off—to *conceive* of such a turning as determined by some facultative force—but equally, he understands—and this, he thinks, is crucial, the hinge on which he's balanced his insurgence from the start—the discernment of one's will, of one's disordered inclinations— disordered into such untoward assurance of a bound—is received by the same means that's always previously taken in...*discerned* a world accounted...

φ

An inexorable regress afflicts every discernment, that such act can't help but determine as its underlying object the action of discernment itself. And as such there is little that discriminates the structure of the consciousness—the *agency*—intrinsic to one's carriage from what that self-same agent must claim for the fulfillment of the claim that follows hence. The necessity most readily called fate when it's concluded—that effectuates acceptance of conditions as received—is the sense of what's internal to one's thinking, the state of that interior subsistence still conditional to choosing, to his having ever had a choice, made previous or...

φ

Everything that comes to him, every twinge and twitter, every act of understanding, every farrowing remainder, every everything discerned is...is made *is* by the posture of the subject that discerns it, the pressing back and into of the seity that gleans it as the inner of an outside whole. Even what one thinks one's ownmost semblance of desires is a force that can't be managed without concurrent relegation to a surface, that in the knowing *of* it is subjected to the same sort of condition by which every other differential predicate is understood distinct, if not...

φ

It is not precisely clear, not precisely an occlusion; he needs not here remark—or it needs no such remarking—that the picture of one's agency most usually assumed...*betokened* through such ardor is not satisfied by realizing the seity that knows itself knows something that's extrinsic; something that remains outside the consciousness that sees it, for whom the vision of such seity is always as an outside that's received...

φ

Alas, he thinks, this might portend the savor of affliction if he could keep it present...make it *inner* to his thinking about anything at present or at all, but the best that he has done...that he *can* do with this premise is to understand his choices as determined, as *preempted*; to take up his position as a *necessary* gull. He thinks he has described the innovation of necessity, of what within his purview, while conceivably exempt...still conceivable as having yet another place and parlance, is by virtue of discernment—his discernment of an outside—deduced as a necessity in full, if not in part. He's not sure why it matters, now that the torrent's over—now that the ache of neck and back and knees has been restored—except that there *is* comfort in believing his position brought upon him, given to him; in thinking that there's nothing else...that nothing else could happen; that everything he's ever thought of doing has led him to this moment, a moment which is more or less the choosing of his next assent to choose...

φ

It's not that he has had no choice, but that such choice is one more form of posed instantiation he understands as equal to his fate. What this insight means—what it could ever *have suggested*—to anyone else...well, he doesn't need reminding that if any such are extant—have *ever* been made subject to this vigorous pursuit—or not, he cannot say...he cannot *know* the difference, acknowledging the prospect still inspires some small measure of relief. It's not that he has put an end to such responsibility—to rejuvenate his innocence, thus to expiate his guilt—though such feeling is a benefit he will not turn aside, or turn against. More readily, he feels he has been freed from the imperatives of purpose—of what he understands as purposes pursued; freed from what might otherwise afflict him in discerning that he has no need to seek a grander end than this he's living, this sundering of certainty—of certain *possibility*— from fate. He feels...he *knows* he's following the path that's set before him, and that alone, and that at last...

φ

He knows he's still presenting what he's recently rejected as though he has established it as undisputed fact—that his giving up of agency is a path to manumission; that acceptance of his course as a *necessity* has freed him from all concern for making the right choice, and that doing so he's countered that same precept, that same station—he's taken back position on the beetling escarpment that establishes the seer as a conscience, thereby birthed *another* new restraint. It's not that he's at ease with such a paradox of portents; this hall of mirrors has done little to distract him from what anyone of similar abilities would presume to think an affect of monition or response. He's freed, he thinks again, by having circumvented freedom, freed by living in his world without...

φ

And so the clumsy query which this incidental inference has compelled into such granular riposte—released, that is, to ask or say...to think or will...*to what*? What is it he can do that he couldn't have before he knew he couldn't rightly think such aims a predicate of choosing, of any *possible* choice? What will he do differently, now that he has this freedom—how would he be different now if he'd possessed it in the past? Such questioning unquestionably contravenes the premise that enticed him to its asking in the first place, from his origin; if this world is his fate, he thinks, then this world is his fate. If freedom is the freedom to do otherwise than anything—to choose one world in particular from those that are expounded in due course—then it's circular to argue that the method of accomplishing such freedom is denial of its presence, of its coming into presence...

φ

He will not here again...not here and not again evade the point of his evasions of the point...It seems to him the problem is in no small part compelled by his mistaking of some contractile sphincter for an egress, for the promise of an *apt* release. Yes, he understands the very first step that one takes beyond the mount of one's encircling meatus may appear to hold the promise of infinite choice, but soon enough the prisoner will be immured within the posture that makes every choice a new form of confinement, another chance to struggle against chance restraints. He is not newly born, he is not less a stranger; his muscles are no stronger, his joints still burn and ache. If there are minor differences that keep his interest longer—that prevent him from descending to the boredom that's his natural state—then well enough. He has again his freedom, but...

φ

It's freedom *from*, not *to*, he thinks—the dative inclination that his vigor can't *not* seek. His necessity...his *capitulation* to necessity is at best…at *least* another skirting of the scruple that pursues him, that sense of the inconsequence of always choosing wrongly which assaults him when he chooses…

φ

If he's chosen then he's always chosen wrongly, he admits. It's plain to him that if his every act is chosen *for* him by the heedless choosing *of* him as the agent of its craft—if everything he is is made discernible as object by virtue of its discharge of the outside of the in…of the *ingressed*—then those aspects that determine his perspective as a jumble of desires are the first order of givenness determined to determine who he is—who he'll *be next*. Who he is is who he'll be, undeterred by his position; he knows that in the end he'll drive his languor towards *some* billet, exceeding all his failed attempts to carry out…to carry off…

φ

And this, it seems to him, is a more reasonable…more *realistic* substitution of his reason for his fate. He's obliged to think he's choosing between standards, between options—options given *to* him without the intimation of a choice. He may adopt some one path over others, but only as it accords with what he's managed to discern within his person—with tastes that, though inside him, he will passively accept. What appeases *through* this kilter is his pleasure in asserting his surrender to velleity as an exploit of discernment, a feat that takes away all sense of agency by claiming for his nature his position between personhood and world. He is not what he is not, he thinks the premise artless; he is not not that callow affectation of a motive that his suffering demands of every affect, every motive…

200

φ

And finally he's found a road to comfort, to relief. It's difficult to accept that he might be accused of brooking such inquiry only for the sake of...*in search of* this result—for this, that is to say, and neither more nor else; that he may have deceived...been *deceptive* in submitting to some end that he thought soothing...that allows a forward surge from his last movement forward...

φ

One might indeed suspect him of pursuing what's most easy, rather than what merely matters most. And what of it; why should he be held back from a principle that others seem to follow with a passion that suggests no other choice? What's wrong with searching out a little bit of comfort? What does he have going that would suffer from such license—the license to crave egress *from this stance*? What imperative to relevance or truth has he rejected? What refusal of the kind has instigated either a dilation in discomfort—in the clench of his position—or some subsequent denial of all access to the problems of the world he's since accepted as advanced? Even if he's made some fleet concession to such easement in the keening cant by which he is disposed to other ends...to come to any posture he can think of as resplendent, does it matter if there's never any consequence to where he's been, or will be next? To where his next has been...

φ

A loss is only real if it's perceived, if it's *resultant*—if one can offer up the possibility of *discernible effect*. Discernible *diminishment* of something one thinks valuable—a loss of what one *wants* to lose might well be called a gain, and so is not the object of this petulant descant. That this is not the case as it occurs to him right now may be confused for consolation—an assertion by which his conscripted purposes *make less*—and so he thinks he ought provide some sort of apologia, some picture of his posture that may serve as a defense. What he remains unsure of—what he still can't *represent*—is that assemblage of a pose that will prove cogent in the face of such desires, a question only possible to answer if he can first identify to whom it will attest. To whom such proof will prove effective...

φ

And *when* he thinks it clearly—more *distinctly*, as a chance receipt—it seems he's only speaking to an archetype, a paragon; that the beau ideal he's speaking to is equal to the beau ideal that's speaking, that has spoken; that it's only to this image of another who has access to the comfort of his...his *polemic* on behalf of present stasis or attempt. He is *as though* another—in his role, if not his glance...he takes on his position as the other placed beside him, the other who can validate his claim to some esteem, to some effect...

φ

In this regard, he thinks he may be censured for his interest in what he'd like to think of as disinterested impulse. He is not at all unwilling to accept as proof what others might find specious, so that each for whom this process is concerned might amble past without a second look. He would like, that is to say, to give up trying to forswear this last remainder of a world he's neither entered nor discerned as *in itself*, but such desire makes capitulation to the absence of desire impossible to sanction—to *conceive of* as resultant, let alone result...

φ

There's no way to transcend such idle foundering in regress—the regress of succumbing to this burden of *attempts*—no matter what the object or the absence of object,
the object or the void put in its place. Inasmuch as there's no
stipulation by which he can...he's *willing* to pass judgment
on the evidence he's giving in support of some familiar
gest, he can always doubt his interest in the witness, in the
testament; there will always be a question that his answer
can't dismiss, or act against...

φ

It is futile, it occurs to him, to bring about a proof of his
disinterest in the proving if he can't recognize another...a
wholly *disinterested* other to whom his act of witness—of
account—can be directed, if not conspicuously addressed.
And even this, he understands, presumes that such a fantasy of otherness is chosen—has been gathered from the
masses of disinterested dissents—for any reason but his
dazed ability to act as validation for the spokesman, for the
speaker; for the prover, just as he has proved to be...

φ

There is perhaps some comfort in realizing that his comfort
doesn't all at once envelop his obligatory shrift. He need
not tell himself he's taken paths that have proved contrary
to his sense of contiguity, that his many inclinations are
both pleasurable and pained, and so suggest he's doing
more than simply following the easy path—his achievements, after all, have hampered any progress in the easing
of his wants. That he would find alternatives more painful
may inspire one to doubt his droll assertion of persistence

unconcerned, but such doubt still goes no way towards a contrary imperative—towards any motive contrary to what he calls…he *claims* to call…

φ

That he has found some pleasure in a truth revealed—a truth *compelled*—does not imply that one truth is more pleasing than another, not from the perspective of his present weal, his present future mold; it may be that such verity is all he's ever after, that sooth has proved a predicate more pleasing to his nature than any proposition that propels him towards escape…

φ

Unable to confirm he hasn't used this *amour propre* in the drawing out of one peculiar end from all the rest—he *hopes*, that is, he finds a way to do so universally, to make sure such advantage is not ever far from use—he can assure himself that what he finds most pleasing often causes him considerable discomfort down the pike. He's well aware the ease that first produced this same reflection on the prospect of his easement has had nothing much to do with his taste for truth; his interest was assuaged by the release from what concerned him, his comfort in realizing that he need not soon concern himself with questions of his freedom as he limps along in search of brace or grip. And the thought that stimulates him to forgo this cruel suspicion—to give himself the benefit of this prodigious doubt—is that on thinking back to what revealed his stricken locus at the finish of his ambit, all evidence seemed directed towards another…towards what appears a mire of *unwitting*—if not precisely other—wants…

φ

He's found some slight relief from what he thought the bonds of servitude—of thralldom to exemption *or* surrender, either way—and as such he is possibly the first mind to find freedom…to escape, he thinks, from personhood by knowing such escape always returns one to confinement in its borders; escape by understanding that there's nothing to escape from, that there's no way to distinguish between being in and out. What matters to him now has nothing left to do with longing—is but another blighted exigence, a sundering from every form of circumspect pursuit; he has no choice but to disburse his groveling attention to the throbbing choke, the choking vent…

φ

There is a sense of weight, he thinks, the weight has been increasing, a fact of sheer sensation…of *discernment* he still doesn't think an attribute of what's within his head or what the means to comprehend it, to feel that space within him as it's filling, as the obviated compass of its surface swells. To make it more confusing, there is something in the nature…in the *character* of the world that has resulted in an increase of its pull upon his purview—the purview set *within* the gibbous knees that frame his view…

φ

He does not know how to discern the setting that surrounds him, that he might soon determine its foundation and its end, although he still believes there's a defensible objective in attempting to consolidate…to *make entire* this unbalanced regress of sensations, and so see what is changing with analogous, perhaps even *reciprocal* effect. If something moves coincident with any other change in nature—is transfigured in some way that's still contiguous with result—then one might well conjecture that those changes are related... are *associated* causally, or are accurately understood effects of the same causal strife...

φ

And so it seems apparent that the increase is concurrent with his quickening decline towards ever deliquescent humus, a movement that itself is only measured...only *measurable* by noticing coincident revisions of perspective, of the view between his legs now so much more of land than sky. The weight within his head, the change within his view, the clench of muscles in the limbs to keep him from a wallow in the muck of marl—all seem in the system and the nature of the same effect, as far as he's concerned, and while such an assumption of the wholeness of the world is a necessity if he still hopes to ascertain...to *think of* any inference as verified *in fact*, it can't reveal what he is looking for, what symptom is more rightly called a class, a class of...

φ

This hardly seems a justified—even *justifiable*—endeavor *or* surrender to observable intent; he has not fashioned any fateful reason to distinguish such elucidated cause when so much else that he's allowed himself to think has been received as it's delivered, with an evident simplicity that can't be reproduced. That can't be faked or taken for some subtlety of parsing; of parsing what appears as an immediate...a manifest...an *ever-present* dissonance—what he understands the nature of his ever-present fix...

φ

He accepts what's given to him, so he thinks it as an ought; he's content with what he's given, so he'll never ask for either more *or* else. Well, that's not quite right, he thinks, he's asking at this moment, if he understands what's happening...what he's asking...what he's *hoping* to continue at this moment...He tries, that is to say, to make his object meet his affect without second thought or first to qualify as a discretion, that he is just a simple soul whose simple aims are met by simple pleasures...by simple pains and pleasures...

φ

For once he will pass over it, for *this* once once and only; he may not have the chance to live so carelessly again. He may not have another chance but that's no proper warrant; his practice of such negligence, while not without attraction, can't draw him from more common cause, when that cause is a manner to maintain his present stance. Still, it's not such grave concern that keeps him from the problem... from trying to push through the bar he's been thrown up against. For him, there is no reason to press forward with analysis if he can't do so with the goal of a more permanent...more assuredly *sustainable* restraint. He simply will not do it; he simply can't be turned if he's not sure of getting something...arriving somewhere...somewhere other than...

φ

That this is the position in which he languishes at present he thinks woefully apparent, but for the sake of something *like* the clarity of purpose he proposes as his warrant he resolves to take a chance...to take his *chances* on what seems to him the folly of restatement, that he might never think to waste his time on it again. Something like, if not precisely. One shouldn't set one's hopes too high…

φ

He's disposed to the belief that both his posture and his bearing are in some way more connected than the disassociation of originary referents would suggest; that the odium of substance—of intractable *equivalence*, in the wake of his submission to a contractile balance—requires the decline of his position in this pageant—his taking up position as a patron or a polyp, a pinion or an involuted gust…He thinks that he has found his way by having his way find him—by *letting* his way find him—as though there were an agency within him that's without…that's within him and without him all the same. Whatever that means. He doesn't know what *that* that means, but knowing that he doesn't care…*not caring* allows him…has allowed him…

φ

He's allowed himself to use this ambiguity because he's sure he'll never make it clearer in the end, that his habit of assuming such a numinous connection between status and position has a history in his life that's impossible to proffer as reversible, as happening *by chance*. This, he thinks, is more than the advantage of some vanity discerned alone by hazarding its affable dissent, that through such contradictory analysis he's able to make explicit under what terms he'll forgo all further study of the issue, accepting just as well what's problematic in that vision, in that purpose and that point. He's come again to some still newly aspirant conclusion by riffling through byways that he knows will be dead ends, but those conclusions are concerned…are only truly *apropos* the standing of his stasis, are not attained or practiced by the forward glance…

φ

And so is his return to the inquiry from which this most contemporary of inquiries was diverted as much of a requirement to the reaching of an end that's more than tangent—that he's devised as some way to avoid his falling head first to the ground. He must discern why he's discerned he's having so much trouble—what hidden force impels his pate into the taffy loam—if he's ever to elude the grand indignity of...of having first to raise himself up from it and restore what he's inclined to think his proper place, his vacant prime. The solution to the problem that he's presently *caught in* is no more difficult than pulling himself upright—than standing up to face his means, to mean his wants in turn—but he's not sure he can do it, that he can bring about...can *motion towards* that scope and stand, the next resumption...

φ

His knees are in such torment, as his thorax at the waste; his ankles are now throbbing just a beat back from his cheeks; his ears are hot, his neck is stiff, his fingers cramped in clenching may soon slip off grimy trousers, and worse than that, than all of that, his vizard—rouged with pits and scrapes—feels as if it carries so much more of this inertial bulge, this static freight...

φ

And that's not everything, he thinks, it's not yet all of his concerns. He knows there must be more—that some interior contortion is still waiting for description—by the pains that come and go across his torso and his loins. He knows that there is more, but not quite how to recognize it, how to bring those blurred conditions into clarity of mind, and in this sense he feels sure that such a thoroughgoing...such *exhaustive* explanation will not prove his path to liberty — the freedom from abatement that his questioning impedes. Better to think long on that original oration, on the one and only focal point of his assured decline; better to submit to what attracts the most attention, that affliction of tumidity that marks his path...his path to fulgent viscus and crepuscular jejunum...his suppliance to scant release, to guts clenched tight...

φ

And so to dream his portless ataraxia to presence, perhaps it's right that he should set his crown on some new throne. Perhaps that he's accustomed to the parlance of reversal, that he has formed a mare's nest of his foretop and his deadened limbs; that he has culled a tel on which to seethe and angle, made stable by his muddle in the press of mucid rime, will let him now continue with his wearying distention — until, that is, he needs again...again to make his move...Forsooth he thinks this new pose transforms tripod into hassock, the inferential anchor of the cosmos it inscribes, as though such fitful posturing of orison and sacrifice can be claimed for a god who's yet to suffer the contumely of an idle oath, a sacred void...

φ

STEVEN SEIDENBERG is the author of *Situ* (Black Sun Lit, 2018), *Null Set* (Spooky Actions Books, 2015), *Itch* (Raw Art Press, 2014), and numerous chapbooks of verse and aphorism. His collections of photographs include *Pipevalve: Berlin* (Lodima Press, 2017) and *Kanazawa Void* (Daylight Books, forthcoming 2018).